Rev. G. H. Wilkinson

Holy Week and Easter

Rev. G. H. Wilkinson

Holy Week and Easter

ISBN/EAN: 9783741194924

Manufactured in Europe, USA, Canada, Australia, Japa

Cover: Foto ©Andreas Hilbeck / pixelio.de

Manufactured and distributed by brebook publishing software
(www.brebook.com)

Rev. G. H. Wilkinson

Holy Week and Easter

HOLY WEEK

AND

EASTER

THE REV. G. H. WILKINSON, M.A.

Author of "Some Week-Days in Lent," "Guide to a Devout Life," "Instructions in the Way of Salvation," etc.

NEW YORK
E. P. DUTTON AND COMPANY
713 BROADWAY
1881

PREFACE.

—o—

THE following pages contain the substance of Addresses delivered in St. Peter's, Eaton Square, in 1872. They are printed from Notes taken at the time by a member of the congregation.

They have been found so helpful, that the Author does not feel justified in withholding them from publication, on account of their obvious and manifold defects.

May the Blessed SPIRIT over-rule what is mistaken, supply what is wanting, and bless what is according to the Mind of GOD !

St. Peter's, Eaton Square.
    Lent, 1880.

HOLY WEEK AND EASTER.

———o———

Monday in Holy Week.

ANY of us who are accustomed to analyze our own consciousness must often have found, that those seasons in which we hoped for a special harvest seemed wasted. We expected so much, and felt that we had gained nothing. We have been disappointed at the end of Lent, Advent, etc.

Often, this may be from *want of preparation* for the blessing. Therefore, on this first day of Holy Week, I wish to help you to prepare for the week on which we are entered.

First of all, then, begin as the Prayer-Book has taught us from childhood, with CONFESSION OF SIN. We have to repeat this again and again; for old sins and old temptations rise up again and again, and Satan blinds our minds

again and again to old truths that we once realized with intensity.

Say to God: "Almighty and most merciful
FATHER, Who only canst make this Holy Week
a blessing to my soul, and Who art more ready
to hear than I am to pray, I have erred and
strayed from Thy ways," etc.

There must be the acknowledgment that we
are wicked; that there are sins—depths of evil
—in us, that we have never yet fathomed. "In
me dwelleth no good thing." Every year, as
the light becomes clearer,—as the knowledge
of our own utter sinfulness grows deeper,—we
learn to see our sin, so as we saw it not in our
earlier spiritual life; we find out sins of which
we were then wholly unconscious. Sin is only
revealed to us little by little, as God sees that
we can bear it. Therefore, we must not be
surprised, if some new aspect of wickedness is
revealed to us; we must acknowledge, to the
end, that God alone knows how wicked we
are.

We must tell our sins to God. We must
acknowledge now, in silence, any special sin,

which is hindering us, at this moment, from communion with God. If you have done any thing wrong this morning, confess it to God. Say: "O my God, I was irreverent;" or: "O my God, I gave way to temper;" or: "I was false; I acknowledge my sin unto Thee."

2. BELIEVE IN OUR LORD JESUS CHRIST. Take home to yourself, as if spoken individually to you, that word of God: "The Blood of JESUS CHRIST cleanseth us from all sin:"— as if you had knelt there,—according to the custom of the Early Church,—before the whole congregation, and, in their hearing, had acknowledged that sin to God; and then, God's Minister had stood up before God, and declared to you God's forgiveness of that sin. Lay hold of that word of God: "Their sins and iniquities will I remember no more." "Thou wilt cast all their sins into the depths of the sea." Watch the circles made on the water, where a stone, a few minutes ago, has fallen; then, all is still. As that stone has sunk, so has God, in virtue of

that once-offered Sacrifice, cast all our sins "into the depths of the sea."

3. PUT YOURSELF INTO THE HANDS OF JESUS CHRIST, for this week; to be taught by Him; to be healed, to be dealt with by Him, as a Living Person, in whatever way He may see fit. At this very time, in that sad week, "the blind and the lame came unto Him in the Temple, and He healed them." And so, you and I may lie at His feet,—blind, lame, leprous, paralyzed, dumb,—to be healed; to be set free to run in the way of His Commandments, to have our eyes opened to see His LOVE, our lips opened to speak His praise. "O LORD, open Thou my lips, and my mouth shall show forth Thy praise."

But, as you do this, guard against a very common snare of Satan. When we start, at the beginning of Holy Week, to seek a blessing, Satan takes care that we shall not get that blessing *consciously.* It often comes, when we feel utterly dead and cold. As a worn-out man, taking a holiday, feels tired all through, and thinks no good has been gained; and yet, on his return to work, is astonished to find in himself more force nerve, health; so, when we are expecting to draw in spiritual health, we often *feel* no benefit at the time: and yet, strength is being really poured in, and fruit comes afterwards, in many a temptation conquered, many a battle won.

Remember, then, that many a Holy Week of conscious weakness may not be a week wasted; only, it is better not to put ourselves into Satan's hands, by being unprepared.

4. THINK FIRST OF CHRIST, NOT SELF. Do not start with the idea of self;—of gaining something—even spiritual blessing—for yourselves; but of honoring our LORD JESUS CHRIST, by following Him, as far as He may allow, in this Week of His suffering. Instead of wasting time in analyzing how far it is our own fault, when we have failed, and feel troubled and fretted by a crowd of trifles,—so small, it may be, that we are ashamed to name them,—let us surrender our spiritual selves to Him. Let us begin by acknowledging that we are sinners, and that it is not for us to say how this Holy Week is to

be used. We simply follow while He leads:
darkly, coldly, it may be—as it was with HIM
a time of darkness; but—*following!* Come here,
to worship, not to have a spiritual feast. Of
·course, if a spiritual feast is provided, you will
thank Him. But, if not, say: "Amen; even
so, FATHER!" Think of HIM, not of self.

5. BELIEVE IN THE HOLY GHOST. Open your
Bible. Read Zech. xii. 10. See how GOD promises the HOLY GHOST to enable us to look on
JESUS, Whom we have pierced. Read St. John
xiv., xv., etc., which brings before us more
fully the work of the HOLY GHOST, as a *Living
Person.* GOD promises the help of the HOLY
SPIRIT, to make us sorry for our sins; to witness
for CHRIST; to give us sympathy with Him; to
help us to follow Him whithersoever He goeth.
The HOLY SPIRIT alone can make the Passion a
reality to us. The HOLY GHOST loves to reveal
JESUS to us. Say to Him: "O GOD, Thou hast
promised to pour upon us the Spirit of grace and
of supplication." Ask, believing in your LORD,
though all may seem unreal to you. Put your-

self into the SAVIOUR's Hands, remembering to honor the HOLY GHOST. Take these passages, and plead them. Say: *"Thou hast promised!"*

THREE THOUGHTS IN CONCLUSION.

(1.) Think of the use you can make of the Collects. Expand them for yourselves; try to get into the spirit of the Church prayers. This week, you will find depths of prayer in the words of the Communion Office. "We are not worthy so much as to gather up the crumbs," etc. Say to Him: "O GOD, I am indeed not worthy! How little I deserve!"

(2.) When you can not feel,—can not pray,—when you find nothing but difficulties and darkness, do not take it for granted that you will not be able to pray, that day. Cast yourself on the HOLY GHOST, "the LORD, and Giver of life!" Say to Him: "O help me to pray!" A direct appeal to the HOLY SPIRIT often ends in the very happiest time.

(3.) Lastly: INTERCESSION.

Ask, this week, for a blessing on the *little children* of the Parish. Ask Him, that some of

these children, as they hear the story of JESUS'
LOVE, may be drawn to Him.

Pray for the *sick and suffering*, here and elsewhere; and for those deprived of outward helps.

Pray for *returning Penitents*. In one sense,
this is praying for ourselves; for all of us, as we
draw near to the Cross of CHRIST, have need to
humble ourselves for our own sins. But especially your prayers are asked for those who are
just *beginning* to turn to GOD. It is so hard for
them ! There are many such in this Parish;—
just beginning to think, with very little sense of
sin as yet, very little power to pray, etc. It is
so hard for them ! The world looks attractive,
and every thing about religion looks so dark and
cold and dull ! And even those among us who
could go among them and try to draw them in
with the intensity of our love, *will* not always do
so. Therefore we need all the more to pray for
them. O that the power of the Passion may
make itself felt on these souls during this Holy
Week !

Pray for the *Clergy;*—for *all* of us. Pray that
GOD will fill our heart with zeal for souls.

Pray for the *whole Church* of CHRIST! And as you pray, think of the great Intercessor within the Veil, ever carrying on the work of Intercession for us, and presenting our prayers to HIS FATHER and our FATHER.

Tuesday in Holy Week.

"THE PLACE WHEREON THOU STANDEST IS HOLY
GROUND."—(Exodus iii. 5.)

AT times like these, there arises an intense
craving for silence. We long to "be still;"
or, if we *must* speak, merely to open the lips to
plead with GOD His ancient promise: "I will
pour upon you the Spirit of grace and of supplication." The instinct of our hearts is for silence, broken only by a few words of earnest
pleading: "Come, HOLY GHOST, our souls inspire! Come, and reveal to us the Love of
CHRIST, which passeth knowledge! Come, and
reveal Him to us, as suffering for us that Agony
and Bloody Sweat, that Cross and Passion!"

We have a longing to "be still:" to let *Him*
speak those last words from Calvary; to picture
to ourselves the Crucifixion; to watch that last
struggle; to hear that last cry; and then, silent-

ly and thankfully, to remind our own hearts of the words spoken to us in the Lesson of this day: "As the Father hath loved Me, so have I loved you; continue ye in My Love." (St. John xv. 9.)

This instinct is not a mere impulse. It becomes stronger, as years go on, and we bring the power of our matured minds to bear upon the scenes which were enacted, in this world of ours, during that first "Holy Week." It is not merely that we are baffled by the old question that arises: "How could a loving GOD permit such suffering? Why must CHRIST die?" We are content to put aside such questions; to acknowledge that they are beyond us. And yet, in the quiet of the early morning, when we are kneeling at that Holy Table, and trying to understand something of this Week of the Passion, we are baffled, perplexed, disappointed. Why is this?

I. It arises, partly, from *the Nature of the Being whose Sufferings we are considering*. In the words of the old Creed which it is the fashion of

the day to disparage, He is "Perfect God, and
Perfect Man." How can we conceive a Being
who is at once God and Man? Hence,—on account of this difficulty,—one half of the Church
ignores the fact of His being "Very God"; the
other half forgets that He is "Very Man."

The result of this first error,—*i.e.*, of ignoring
the Godhead of Christ,—is an irreverent famil-
iarity; thinking of Him as if He were one of
ourselves; talking to Him, without the reverence
due to One Who is so far above us!

On the other hand, the result of ignoring His
Humanity, and therefore forgetting His Human
Sympathy, as bone of our bone, and flesh of our
flesh, is this :—the heart, longing for a Mediator,
is obliged to find for itself another than Christ ;
and is driven to seek, in the Virgin Mary, and
the Saints in Paradise, the filling of the supposed
void, in the Incarnate God! We long for One
nearer to us than the Living God ; and if we are
not allowed to feel the Human Sympathy of
Christ, His Sympathy with all but sin, in our
nature,—the longing is supplied by Mariolatry,
or Idolatry in one or other of its varied forms.

We are therefore obliged to acknowledge, in the Holy Week, that this is "holy ground;" that our faculties are limited; and then try to correct the mistake on either side, by thinking of our LORD JESUS CHRIST at one time, as Man, and at another time, as GOD.

(1.) When inclined to be too familiar, we must dwell on the Godhead of our LORD; we must think of Him, surrounded by the thousands and tens of thousands of angels.

(2.) When we kneel before Him, appalled by the sense of our sin, guilt, and helplessness, and seem so far from Him, that the thought of Him in His glory, as the Centre of the universe, frightens us, and sends us away from Him,— then, we must turn to look at Him as One Who has touched us with a human Hand, and in Whom the human Heart is beating with a human Sympathy.

II. This limitation of our faculties strikes us in yet another way. Time and Space are the moulds in which our ideas are formed; the moment we pass out of those limits, we feel lost.

Beyond the limits of the visible world, our ideas are vague and shadowy.

Consequently, the old Gospel of 1800 years ago loses much of its blessing; the Passion of our LORD loses much of its power over us.

We can think of JESUS, sympathizing with Martha and Mary at Bethany; of His tender love, His words of mercy to the poor woman kneeling before Him: "Go in peace!" We can watch Him, as on last Sunday we read and heard of Him, with the human tears streaming down His Face, as He wept over the city that He loved. All this, we can understand and realize.

But the moment we try to follow Him into the world unseen, our powers seem paralyzed; all becomes vague and unreal. It seems to us impossible to think of "this Same JESUS," being sorry when He sees us sinning, and glad when we do better; pained when we transgress; grieved at our backslidings; sorrowing over us, when He sees us purchasing Hell for ourselves, although He died to procure us an entrance into Heaven. Thus, words like these: "Why persecutest thou ME?" have no meaning to us, practically.

And yet,—next to the Atonement itself,—*the* thought that gives me courage and strength is this. The husband, when obliged to leave his wife in a far country, to go home and make ready for her, does not forget her trials and sorrows, because he is himself at rest and peace. On the contrary, if the tidings reach him, that his wife is suffering, or that she is sinning,—forsaking the old friends who did her good, becoming light and flippant, and seldom seen at Holy Communion, he is grieved and sad. And so, I love to think of my Lord,—the Head of the Mystic Body, of which I am but a weak and tempted member; the true, heavenly Bridegroom, unseen, and yet so near; loving the Bride for whom He has gone to prepare a place; loving the Church whom He has left behind to struggle and suffer, assailed and often vanquished by that Spirit of Evil with whom He Himself fought in Gethsemane.

I love to think of Him, longing for the time when the struggle will be over; looking for the Day when He may come back to His spiritual Bride, and present her to His Father, arrayed in her beautiful garments, and bring her to His own Home, in that bright and happy Land where every tear shall be wiped away.

I love to think of Him, waiting for the Day when the whole number of the Redeemed shall be gathered in, and "He shall see of the travail of His Soul, and shall be satisfied;" when He shall no longer have to look down and see the members of His Body, suffering, tempted, often falling; trying to get as much as they can of the world which crucified Him,—bargaining how *little* they may give to Him, and how much they may keep for themselves, and yet be saved at last!

I love to think of my LORD, waiting, in sympathy with His Church on earth, when she says: "Ashes to ashes, dust to dust;" beseeching Him, shortly to accomplish the number of His Elect, and to hasten His Kingdom: waiting, in sympathy with the souls in Paradise, as the cry ascends into His ears: "How long, O LORD, how long?" I love to think of Him, watching lest I come short of my glorious calling; waiting for the day when I shall see Him face to face.

This it is, that nerves me for Mission-work;—
not merely that the Gospel may be preached,
and souls saved; but that the time may be short-
ened during which our LORD has to wait, till
"He shall see of the travail of His Soul, and
be satisfied." This it is, that makes us pray:
"Come, LORD, come quickly;"—the longing
that HE may see His people gathered in; the
one glorious Church, for which He agonized,
fasted, wept, prayed; and for which He still feels
a sympathy which,—so far as *we* can understand
it,—none can feel, except accompanied by pain;
a sympathy which none but those who have suffered themselves can feel, as He watches her falling short of the glorious privileges to which she
is called, and which He purchased for her at
such a price !

But our faculties are limited; we feel how
powerless we are, fully to grasp the thought of
the Human Heart of JESUS,—His tender, un-
failing love and sympathy; "the Same, yesterday, and to-day, and forever ! "

III. Once more. This instinct for silence,

this longing to "be still," in the Holy Week, arises from yet another source.   It arises, partly, from *a limited understanding of the minds of others.*

It is a large subject on which we have to dwell, this week,—the Passion of our LORD; and the teaching which helps one soul to realize it, is sure to hinder others.

It is actual pain, to many, to listen to any details of our LORD's physical sufferings.   To those who have never endured pain, physical suffering seems a kind of degradation.   *Mental* torture, *spiritual* agony,—these they can understand, as elements of His Suffering; these seem to them worthy of the GOD-MAN!   But the bodily agony of the Crucifixion,—this seems to them unworthy to be dwelt upon.   Those who speak thus have probably never experienced the benumbing, paralyzing effect of mere physical agony, upon the mind and soul.

Others dislike the subject, from the very intensity of their love.   Just as a wife would rather die, than listen to the details of the tortures endured by her husband when he fell into the hands of some savage tribe, so the Christian, truly loving CHRIST, may feel that he can not bear to listen to a recital of the pains He suffered; the pierced Hands, or the wounded Side.

And yet, those very details of the physical suffering,—of the crown of thorns, of the Blood-drops streaming from the Brow, of the cruel robe cast over the half-healed wounds, of the pierced Hands, of the cry, "I thirst,"—those very details have won many a soul, have helped many a weary sufferer to endure patiently. The mere fact that JESUS felt weary,—has helped many a worn-out worker. The mere fact that JESUS knew what it was to be struck on the Face, has helped many a boy to bear a blow patiently. The fact that JESUS hungered, has helped a man before now, to die rather than steal. The fact that JESUS passed the night in the cold, shivering, and in pain, without sleep, has helped many a poor girl to say, from that couch which she could never hope to leave: "Even so, FA-THER! Thy SON suffered; I will suffer with Him. If it be possible, take away this cup from me! If not, Thy Will be done!" The very same physical details of the Passion, which only pain one heart, brings comfort to another.

I return to the thought with which I began. Our natural instinct for silence on these subjects is confirmed by the experience of after years. And therefore, the Clergyman who is obliged to stand up and speak to his people, at such a time, can only cast himself on the HOLY GHOST, and on the prayers of his people, at the threshold of the Holy Week, as he feels that the place where he is standing is indeed "holy ground"; praying the HOLY GHOST to suggest the thoughts that will comfort and cheer, and to help him to clothe those thoughts in reverent words; and yet, to save him from keeping back, through fear of irreverence, from one poor tempted child of GOD, one crumb of comfort that GOD would supply. He casts himself on GOD the HOLY GHOST, to Whom nothing is impossible, to make this Holy Week a week of blessing to many a soul.

Thank GOD, some of the reflections that suggest themselves are clear enough.

1. Our LORD JESUS CHRIST came down to

earth, underwent the Agony of Gethsemane, and hung on the Cross of Calvary, "to seek and to save that which was *lost.*"

Did *you* ever feel "lost"? Have you known what it is to stand before God, overwhelmed with the sense of guilt, crying: "God be merciful to me, a sinner?" It is a strange truth, of which we have been lately reminded, that "we may sing Hosannas, and chant praises to the Lord, and yet never have bowed before Him as a Saviour!" O that God may write that truth in the hearts of my people! For there are many here to-night, who have learned a great deal, and yet have never learned that they are "lost"; and who therefore have never felt the joy and peace of being saved,—the comfort of the soul that can thank God for deliverance, through Jesus Christ.

2. Our next thought is a simple and practical one. Our Lord came "*to seek and to save* that which was lost." Therefore, if we wish to be like Christ, *we also must try to seek and save the lost.* This we can do, in many ways.

(*a*) We can do it in the lowest and easiest way, by helping those Institutions which are intended to assist those who are, technically and emphatically, the "lost."

(*b*) But there are other ways. A man can often save another man, by running the risk of being thought a hypocrite, and speaking out boldly the truth that he knows by experience;— by telling others that he himself "was lost, and is found;" that there is a Saviour for the lost!

(*c*) There is another way; one that is much wanted. In our own streets and even in our own homes, can be found many who, in GOD's sight, are as truly "lost," as the poor creature who drowns herself underneath the bridge, because life is no longer bearable. Happy is the family, in which there is not *one* "lost" soul; not one soul which, if called to-night to meet its GOD, would hear the word: "Depart!" And when the poor frivolous girl, or the worldly young man, in one of these homes, wishes to lead a new life,—what is the position in which such a one is placed? The people in the "world" from which they are trying to escape are very pleasant! There is the merry laugh, the round of amusement; and if the young man

has dark hours, alone, he drowns them in drink,
or the poor girl drowns them in "pleasure,"
and on the whole, they contrive to be not very
miserable! The preacher says to them: "Escape for thy life;" and the young man, or the
young girl, says: I "*will* escape! I will arise,
and go to my FATHER, and will say unto Him,
I have sinned."

Have you ever thought of the solitary position
in which such a one is placed? The old worldly
friends laugh at the change. "They shall put
you out of their company." And even religious
people do not give them the welcome they yearn
for.

There may sometimes be wisdom in this.
For there. are only *some* who dare do what
JESUS did for others' sake,—"eat and drink
with publicans and sinners." Every one knows
the plague of his own heart; it is not safe, for all.

But, thank GOD, there are many in this church,
who *can* stretch out the hand of fellowship to the
"lost," living round their own doors, or at their
own firesides; to those who, with every thing
this world can give, it may be, are yet "lost,"

in God's sight. The mother can shield her
daughter, when trying to escape from the world-
liness that she feels will kill her spiritual life.
The sister can help her young sister, when,
after her Confirmation, she says: "No more of
the world, for me; Jesus Christ must have *all*
my heart." Those who are blessed with happy
homes can open their doors to the returning
wanderer: they can show, by the bright look,
the happy smile, the loving sympathy, that they
still look on her as a sister, as a "Temple of
the Holy Ghost," and as a fellow-member of
that Church which, following the Footsteps
of her Lord, goes forth "to seek and to save
that which was lost."

God grant that this may be one result to-
day, of our special Intercessions for "Returning
Penitents!"

3. If the Holy Spirit has been using my
voice to-night, I know that He, Who loves
Jesus Christ, and loves to testify to Him, will
have anticipated, in many hearts, this last
thought. After dwelling thus on the Passion

of our LORD, can we go back and *bargain* with
Him, as we have so often done: "What is the
smallest amount of church-going, of prayer, of
study of Thy Word, of meditation, of Holy Communion, that will do? What is the *least* that
Thou wilt accept? How much *must* I surrender
to Thee?"

No! The thought that fills your hearts—*now*
at least, (I can feel it by an electric sympathy,)
whatever it may be to-morrow—is this:

"Love so amazing, so Divine,
Demands my soul, my life, my all!"

LORD, we *wish* to be better; we desire to give
our whole heart to Thee. Make the resolve a
real one! Give us strength to yield ourselves to
Him Who loved us and gave Himself for us; and
Who, when we were "lost," came down from
Heaven to seek and to save us.

Wednesday in Holy Week.

"RISE, LET US BE GOING."—(St. Matt. xxvi. 46.)

THE first step necessary, for every soul, is that which leads it to the knowledge of itself, and of CHRIST, as its Saviour. We have to learn that we are "*lost.*" We have also to learn, that by GOD's boundless mercy, we are *saved*, with a present salvation. Though we may yet be cast away and lost, before another year or month, if we do not abide in the Vine, we ought to know, that if we die to-night, or if CHRIST should come back to-night, we are saved.

Till these two steps—which are, in fact, *one*— have been taken, any thing like steady progress is impossible. There may be fitful starts, earnest longings to be better; but steady progress is impossible, till we have believed in JESUS CHRIST.

If I speak to *one* to whom all this is a matter

of tradition only, not of conscious experience, I would ask that one, to-night, on his knees, to put the question to himself, or ask GOD to answer it: "What shall I do to be saved?" Say to HIM: "O my GOD, if I have never yet felt it, show me that I am lost! Show me how I can be saved!"

If any of you are striving to enter in at the strait gate, do not be disheartened. It is very strait, to some! Satan will let you do much, —a great deal of work, and prayer, and meditation; he will let you come to church, even to Holy Communion,—any thing but simply believe in JESUS CHRIST, and pass into liberty. Satan will stand before the strait gate; he will do *any thing* to prevent your coming to JESUS CHRIST. Do not lose heart. "Seek, and ye *shall* find. Knock, and it *shall* be opened unto you."

But when that first step has been taken,—when once we have passed through the strait gate, and are in the narrow way, we are sure to be confronted with the Passion of CHRIST.

Sooner or later, it *must* encircle us. At some time or other, in some way or other, the Passion of JESUS CHRIST encircles every one who has passed through the strait gate.

To those still outside,—to those living a carnal, self-seeking life, "the Passion" may seem a vague, unmeaning mystery. But, sooner or later, to all who have really entered on the narrow way, rich and poor, old and young, the Passion becomes a very solemn mystery, a sober reality

It finds us out in different ways: in doubt and darkness; in bodily weakness; in failure of mental power; in the yearning to do what we can not accomplish; in disappointments, unkindness, etc. The ways are infinite! Many who have never passed beyond the threshold of home, never gone out to struggle with the outward world, have carried the Cross, in their quiet home life.

But Suffering is only one side of life. There are others who are met by the Passion of JESUS CHRIST, in the life of ACTION.

The cry comes into the inmost heart, "Follow thou ME;" and they can not choose but listen, and follow whithersoever the Voice leads.

Among the Alps, from time to time, in the early morning, we part from some one, unnoticed before, prepared to scale the highest peak. As noon draws on, they tell us that he is on yonder height. We see it glittering in the sunlight, as we watch through the glass. All is dim at first, but presently we see clearly. We see him scaling some crag, far above us. And then, another form becomes visible;—that of his Guide. We see that Guide, just one step in front, as he cuts one standing-place at a time in the solid ice with his strong axe, as they mount up, step by step. Then we see our friend place his foot, firmly and carefully, in that standing-place. There is a pause; another step higher, in the ice. We seem almost mounting up with him, in the intensity of our sympathy. At times, he is lost to our view: but as the hours roll on, we see him patiently rising, struggling up the height, far above us, where the atmosphere is clear,—the air pure! The scorching sun is beating down on that blistered face, but still he is struggling up.   Farther and farther from us, on and on he goes, with the Guide still before him, till at last that Guide has led him to the top of the Alpine height.   He is hidden from our sight, as the cloud descends upon it; but—he has scaled the height !

So has it been, in every age and land, since the Cross was raised on Calvary.   One after another, previously unnoticed in the crowd,—one, in the Church or family,—one after another hears the cry borne to the inmost heart, as on the night-breeze, in hours of quiet meditation; and the Voice says: "Follow thou Me."   And that young man, or that girl, passes silently away,—away from friends and home, from earthly love, from all that they hold dear, to follow, step by step, so long as life shall last, their Guide, the Lord Jesus, up those mountain heights that lead to Heaven.   We watch them, it may be, for many a year, as they toil on; and then, they are lost to sight; for they have entered beyond that bright cloud, where the eye is powerless to follow.

Such is the effect of the Passion, in developing the life of self-sacrifice. Such was its effect on St. Paul; and on men like Henry Martyn, or Bishop Patteson, in our own day. In some form or other, be it in the active or in the suffering life, the PASSION of the LORD JESUS CHRIST has a mighty power over the souls of men.

The question for us, my brethren, is this. How shall we make it a practical power for ourselves? .

Bidding farewell to sentimental dreamings over Gethsemane and Calvary, let us try to realize our position, as individuals, in the sight of GOD. Let us try to imagine ourselves passed away from earth, and looking down on some one else, in our position, with the same surroundings, tempted with the same temptations, burdened with the same responsibilities. And then, let us ask: What are the most likely temptations, the most likely diseases, for that soul?

Having thus found out the "disease," *i.e.*, having found out to what sins and temptations we are most liable—let us go to the Life of our

LORD, which culminated in the Passion, and note the "antidote" for that disease. Let us take a note-book; and on one side, write: "*My* temptation, in this age, and in these circumstances, and with this temperament, is—such a one." And then, on the other side, let there be written an analysis of that part of the Passion, by which it can be remedied. So shall we bring into our system a mighty tonic, from the Blood that flowed from the Pierced Side of our LORD on Calvary.

Let me illustrate my meaning; confining my remarks, to-day, to the life of ACTION.

I. In such an age as this, more or less artificial, it is especially difficult to realize that *we are individual souls*, standing alone before GOD; individually created, redeemed, baptized into the Church of CHRIST; the Cross marked on our individual foreheads; and that we must "appear before the Judgment-seat of CHRIST" as individuals, to give an account of our own life,—not of that of our friends. Every reflecting mind must have felt the danger of forgetting our individuality.

This is a very subtle temptation; because the love of popularity arises from a tendency in human nature that, in itself, is most desirable; *i.e.*, the love of sympathy. The child who does not care for the opinion of others has generally something lacking in its character.

In an age like this, I repeat, it is difficult to realize that we are standing alone before GOD, from morning to night, in the solitary grandeur, or the solitary degradation, of our individual being; in the sight of One Who knows all, Who searches the thoughts of the heart, and records in His Book all that vanishes like the early dew from our own fading memory. It is very difficult to realize that GOD sees *me*, and that I shall stand before Him, one day, alone.

We live too much in the opinions of those around us. We dislike to be singular; we are afraid of being thought foolish,—afraid of making mistakes. So, we write on one side of the page: "LOVE OF POPULARITY."

Now, what is the Antidote, in the life of JESUS CHRIST?

We see Him beginning life with that grandest

of utterances: "I must be about My FATHER's business." In Manhood, we see Him still with that motto: "I muŝt be about My FATHER's business." "Rise, leṭ us be going !" Going, it may be, to Jerusalem, to be crucified: but still, it is "My FATHER's business."

And then, in this culminating week of His Passion, we see Him, Very Man, with His living, human sympathies; shrinking, with all the sensitive and highly strung nerves of His Human Nature, from being left alone in His agony; shrinking from being misunderstood; longing for sympathy (Ps. lxix. 8–20). We see Him going on calmly, in this way of sorrows, though all the religious world was denying Him: though He was called a traitor, a blasphemer ! Think of it, you who know what loyalty means ! All the *religious* world was against Him,—speaking of Him as One by Whom God was dishonored, One Whom God had forsaken !

Think of Him thus, and remember that He was "Very MAN;" His bodily weakness, crushing all strength in His Human Soul ! Left alone; with all His longing for human sym-

pathy,—His deep Love for humanity ! Obliged
to go up that Way of Sorrows, to go steadily forward, to be nailed to that Cross, and to die in
the face of the multitude as a traitor and a blasphemer ! O God, what must this have been,
to Him Who was Thy well-beloved Son ! Help
us to realize something of that Passion, for Jesus
Christ's sake !

We kneel down, and gaze on that Life. We
see it in its completeness, lived as an *individual*
Life before God. And we rise from that contemplation, and say: "God helping me, from
this day I live *as in the sight of my God,*—for
what God can give, not for what man can give,
of praise or blame. I, too, must henceforth
be 'about my Father's business.'"

The Antidote has flowed in; we go forth,
strengthened by the Passion of Jesus, applied to
the life of Action.

II. If it is a temptation, in this age, to be
artificial, to live in a crowd, another danger is—
Luxury. (I am speaking to those who really
want to live for God). This danger, like the

Love of Popularity, is a very subtle one; and for the same reason: that all which nurses in us an effeminate spirit of self-pleasing, and self-indulgent habits, is generally quite harmless, in itself; springing from a natural love of refinement which is not merely innocent, but an immense blessing, given to us by GOD. Taste, refinement,—the power of appreciating all that is beautiful to the eye, or charms the ear,—is not wrong ! The taste for such things is one that JESUS Himself must have shared. It must have been a great trial to Him, to see the coarseness of those who were linked with Him in His Human Life. He would have entered, with us, into the beauty of all that charms the ear and delights the eye. So it is dangerous, from the very fact of its being so harmless in itself. We hardly realize, till we are deprived of our ordinary comforts, how much we depend on them; —going a little longer than usual without food; a less comfortable bed; etc., etc. When we are robbed of any of our comforts, we find how much we depended on them, even in our religious life. We can not enjoy life,—we can not

even pray, or read,—without our comforts !
We find that, almost unknown to ourselves, we
become effeminate, soft, self-pleasing.

So we take our book, and we write on one
side: SOFTNESS; LOVE OF EASE; want of strong
backbone: a danger to which we—in this nine-
teenth century, are specially exposed.

And then we ask: How shall I get the Antidote to this disease, from the Life, concentrated in the Passion, of my LORD? How shall
I find the Antidote, in this week of His Suffering?

Let us kneel down, and try to realize the
events of that Thursday night and Friday morning. We have followed Him in His earlier life;
but this Week seems,—if I may so call it,—the
very essence, the climax, of that Life of self-de-
nial. Reverently let us follow Him.

"He riseth from supper," in that Upper
Chamber. Follow Him; and remember that
He was Very MAN,—His Godhead practically
put aside. (I am not speaking theologically).
"He saved others, Himself He can not save !"
In one sense, this was true. By the law of His

Incarnation, He *could* not save Himself. Therefore, as real MAN, walking out from that Upper
Room,—as really as any of us have walked out,
any quiet evening,—He goes forth, Very Man,
a real, living Man, with His friends, that moon-
light evening, and enters the garden of Gethsemane. There we see Him fall on His Face,
in the intensity of His Agony: and there we
see Him strengthened by the Angel sent from
Heaven, not to lighten His sufferings, but to
help Him to bear yet more. We see Him
nerved afresh for the renewed struggle; strengthened by the Angel, to bear what GOD wills. We
seem to hear Satan whisper, in that hour of bodily weakness: "Call for twelve legions of Angels,
and they shall deliver Thee!" We seem to hear
His answer: "How then shall the Scriptures be
fulfilled, that thus it must be? The cup which
My FATHER hath given Me, shall I not drink it?"

Watch Him, coming back three times for human sympathy from the friends whom He loved,
and finding none! Watch Him, in that struggle of the physical system,—returning, alone, to
the agony of prayer; the Body exhausted, the

Mind harassed, the Spirit crushed; and nothing given Him wherewith to bear it, except that Human Will, which is given to us also;—crushed with suffering, yet resolved to yield itself to the Living GOD; resolved not to flinch one step from the path which His FATHER had given Him to tread.

Think of Him, standing as Very Man, in Gethsemane, confronting the soldiers sent with swords and weapons to take Him. See Him, "bound!"

Follow Him in the early morning (at 2 or 3 A.M.), led to Annas, first; His bands loosed for a time, but standing firm, still and solemn, "about His FATHER'S business."

See Him, bound again, (about 3 A.M.,) taken to Caiaphas. Watch Him, standing before the High Priest: falsely accused, blindfolded, mocked, insulted, buffetted, jeered, spit upon, struck with their hands! Then see Him, (about 6 A.M.,) before the Sanhedrim;—then, dragged to Pilate; —to Herod;—to Pilate again. Watch Him, all that Thursday night, with no refreshment, no rest, no food: and yet, Very Man, with nothing but that Human Will, and that help of the Blessed SPIRIT, which GOD has given to you and to me !

See Him, on the Way of Sorrows! HE felt, so as never man felt, what it was to be stripped, exposed, mocked;—led out to die, without the opportunity of explaining even to the poor women who followed Him, that He was not the traitor, the blasphemer, the GOD-forsaken One, that they said He was. True to the motto of His Life, "Rise, let us be going," see Him going on, to be nailed to that Cross !

From 9 to 12, see Him hanging there, with no support for that weary Head; yet resolute, because GOD the FATHER willed it;—*feeling* the pain, the scorn, the weakness, the exhaustion, the depression, as you and I would have felt it, yet *resolved* not to listen to one whisper of Satan, to call for those legions of angels; not to listen to one whisper of that soft, self-pleasing nature which so often leads *us* astray; not to "come down from the Cross," by the exercise of His Divine Power. He had been trained in the school of suffering, from Nazareth to Calvary;

He had "learned obedience by the things which He suffered" (Heb. ii. 10; v. 8).

Then, from 12 to 3, came the last great trial, when GOD did really seem to have forsaken Him. But still, firm to the end, He who began His Life with, "I must be about My FATHER's business," ended it with "It is finished." "FATHER, into Thy Hands I commend My Spirit."

When, therefore, we have sunk—as we all do, at times—into that effeminate condition, that "love of listless ease," caring for nothing, if only we may not be worried, at home or elsewhere,—then, if GOD helps us to meditate on the Passion, to fix our eyes on the Sufferings of JESUS, in that Human Nature of His, we rise up, strong. We have found the Antidote for the disease, in the PASSION of our LORD.

And so, from that Cross and Passion, whether tempted by the love of popularity, or by the love of ease, we draw a supernatural force, to apply to the whole life of Action.

Does this seem hard teaching? Does the way look too difficult? It may sound hard. But I remember, when that Alpine traveller came back, and we asked: "Was it worth the trouble?"—how his eyes flashed back the answer, even before his lips spoke: "Yes! I have been up *there!*"—as he pointed to that little mountain peak, peaceful in the evening light. He had conquered!

It would not be true to say that it is *not* hard, when trying to break loose from Satan, trying to conquer the old nature. It *is* hard; it is a difficult road; hard to flesh and blood.

But Satan deceives us with a *half* truth, when he tells us of the difficulties of the way. He leaves out of sight this other half of the truth,—that we are not left alone, to tread that road; that He Whom we serve is no grudging Master, asking of us bricks without giving the straw; but that, like the Alpine Guide, CHRIST goes before us, step by step; never giving us more to do or bear than we *can* do or bear; never asking of us one step, before giving strength for it. Satan tells us not of Jesus,—of the joy of His Presence, of the happiness of serving Him.

Satan never tells us of the happy thrill that

goes through the young man, when he had almost yielded himself to sin, but has, by the help of JESUS, crushed the lower nature. He tells us not of that young girl's joy, when others are gone to the merry dance, and she is left alone, because she feels that, however innocent for others, GOD has told her that it would not be good for *her.* Satan tells us not of the joy of that heart, when JESUS comes and speaks to her, as when He came over the hills to Mary of Bethany, and gave her a joy that none of the festive gatherings of Jerusalem could have given.

We are following no hard Master. "The Love of CHRIST *constraineth* us." We live for Him Who died for us! We are following One Who loved us unto death, and Who gives us power to fight and conquer. "Lo, I am with you alway. My grace is sufficient for thee."

That is the blessing of speaking to you, who are baptized, and beginning to stir up the Gift of GOD which is in you. That is the comfort to us, in our dark hours; that the CHRIST Who says, "Follow Me," gives the strength to follow. "I can do all things, through CHRIST which strengtheneth me." "Riše, let *us* be going," we hear Him say; and the power comes.

Rise up, then, ye men and women, and especially ye that are young; rise up, and be about your FATHER's business! It is a glorious life, a noble life, of which the bare outline has been drawn to-day;—a life not yet realized in its fulness, by any of us. Begin, this Holy Week. Drink into your souls, this Holy Week, the Passion of JESUS; and you shall know what is meant by "THE POWER OF THE PASSION, applied to the life of Action."

Thursday in Holy Week.

"MY SON, DESPISE NOT THOU THE CHASTENING OF THE LORD, NOR FAINT WHEN THOU ART REBUKED OF HIM."—(Heb. xii. 5.)

"THE power of the Passion of JESUS, as applied to the life of Action:"—this was our subject yesterday.

The underlying thought was this. As members of CHRIST,—because of the invisible but real union by which we are joined to JESUS CHRIST, and the mysterious in-dwelling of the HOLY GHOST,—we have the power given to us of drawing in, from the Incarnate GOD, strength for our daily life. The HOLY SPIRIT takes the Words of CHRIST, and the Works of CHRIST,— the garments, as it were, in which His Divine Nature was shrouded,—and shows them unto us: and we find them impregnated with a Divine electricity, which, if we wait long enough, gazing on that Life, and drinking in those Words, af-

fects the highest part of our being.   As we meditate on the Passion, life flows in, through those
wounds by which Humanity is healed.

We saw that—in order to use this power—we
may write on one side of our book:—"the Disease;" on the other, "the Antidote:" in other .
words, (1) the temptation to which we are especially exposed; (2) that side of the Passion of
CHRIST, by which the temptation may be over-
come, the disease remedied.

For instance, if tempted,—as all of us are
tempted, at times, to lose our individuality in a
crowd; or if tempted to a love of ease; the Antidote is found by gazing on that earnest Life, beginning with: "I must be about My FATHER'S
business;" and persevering in that steadfast resolve of His Human Will, until the Human
Spirit which His Father had given Him was
again commended to His FATHER'S keeping,
and His work was "finished."

By the marvellous power with which every
utterance of our LORD is gifted, the text of yesterday can be applied, as we have seen, to any
great crisis of life, and to its smallest detail.

"*Rise, let us be going!*" A man who has formed the habit of contemplating the earnest, resolute Life of Him into Whose Name we are baptized, finds a mighty power flowing into his spirit, enabling him to sacrifice ease, comfort, home, life itself, that he may live as JESUS lived, and die as JESUS died. He feels the power of the Passion of JESUS, applied to the life of sacrifice. And the same text can make the poor boy, or the delicate girl, having decided, overnight, what is the proper time to rise (be it 6 A. M. or 10), rise from the bed of sloth, at the first moment. They have learnt how to apply it to the *baby*-detail of not lying dawdling in bed, a quarter of an hour too long. They have learnt the power of that Life of CHRIST, to transfigure common details in the light of the Cross.

To-day, we will take the same thought, and apply it to the other side of human existence,— the life of SUFFERING.

To many of you, thank GOD, these words have no meaning, thus far;. they are only an idea,—a sentiment. But, sooner or later, suffering will find us all out. The thorns are not yet eradicated from the Garden of the LORD; they never will be, till CHRIST returns in glory. In some form or other, suffering must find us out.

The forms in which it may encircle us are various. It may be bodily weakness: the feeling that *will* come to all who do not die early, that their bodily vigor is not what it was; that the brain is beginning to strike work; that they are more easily depressed; that fatigue has become more the normal feeling of their life; that "trifles light as air," yet depressing if daily repeated, are telling upon them. Or it may be home troubles: want of sympathy, misunderstandings, anxieties, disappointments, loneliness. However little of a trial it may seem to others, to us it is a trial;—GOD *knows* we feel it !

Or it may be *spiritual* trial,—perpetual failures, perplexities, never knowing whether or not you are doing right; loss of GOD's conscious Love, etc.; trials which, if once tasted, we never forget on earth: that long, dreary, wilderness-life, when GOD seems far off ! Each of us who have known such trial, can fill up the outline.

And there are some who seem especially marked out for sorrow. Longing for love and sympathy, they are left, lonely, dark, desolate; tempted to covet what GOD has not given, and to look with envy on the happiness of others. They have none but GOD to look to, and perhaps do not yet know the Love of GOD!

GOD alone knows *how* sorrow will come; but it *will* find us out. Like children playing on the seashore, we rejoice when the castles that we have built on the sand have been left by one wave; we rejoice, and go on building; we think that the waves will never wash those castles quite away. But that "cruel crawling foam" comes slowly and surely onward, nearer and nearer, as we move from rock to rock, till our castles are swept away, and we find ourselves encompassed by the rising tide. "Man is born unto trouble." "The fool hath said in his heart, there is no GOD;" but none has said, there is no sorrow.

The question which we would try to answer to-day, is this: How shall I gain strength to bear my suffering,—be that suffering small or great, as the world may judge,—from the Passion of my Incarnate LORD?

But first, I would remind you of the thought which Satan tries so hard to banish from our minds, because He knows that in that thought is power. He with whom we are dealing, this Week, is Very MAN as well as Very GOD. The sufferings that we are contemplating this Week, are the sufferings of One Who, although He was Very GOD as well as Very MAN, never used the power of His Godhead for Himself. The only effect of His Godhead was to aggravate the sufferings of His Human Nature:—that nervous sensitiveness, that exquisite refinement, the nerves quivering under the coarse taunt;—those manifold sufferings which we have tried to realize, in quiet hours.

Lay hold, for a few moments, on this thought. JESUS CHRIST was emphatically "the Truth." Exaggeration was impossible, in Him. Our words may sometimes out-run our feelings; but He used the very words that expressed what was passing in His inmost Heart. And this JESUS CHRIST, Who was "the Truth," tells

us Himself that He was "exceeding sorrowful,
even unto death" (St. Matt. xxvi. 38). He
would not disguise the pain that He felt. He
was great enough not to be ashamed of His
tears. He was great enough to acknowledge
that He felt pain, as pain; humiliation, as humiliation; that He was "exceeding sorrowful,
even unto death."

Let the words fall into thy heart, my brother,
to be treasured up for hours when they will be
needed !

We read that He was "troubled in spirit;"
"sore amazed;" "very heavy !" (St. John xiii.
21. St. Mark xiv. 33). The words express
what Elijah felt under the juniper tree—the utter
stupefaction of pain, weariness, and depression;
Body, Soul, and Spirit, crushed beyond what
they could bear; so that an angel had to come
and strengthen Him, that He might be able to
bear the agony which yet awaited Him. "If it
be possible, take away this cup from me," He
prayed in Gethsemane. And as He hung on
that Cross, He cried: "My GOD, My GOD, why
hast Thou forsaken Me?"

Such are the words which JESUS CHRIST used, to express what passed through that Human Heart of His, in the Week on which we are entering.

With this thought, then, clearly driven into our inmost being, that He on Whom we are gazing is Very GOD, and Very MAN,—a real Human Being, Who would use His Godhead to pour life into *us*, but not to save Himself,—we return to the question: *How are we to meet the temptations of Suffering, in the power which comes from the Passion of Jesus Christ ?*

How ? Precisely as in the life of Action. Ask yourself: "What are my special *Dangers*, in Suffering ?" Write the answer, on one side of your book. And then: "What *Remedy* can I find, in the Passion of my LORD ?"

The first Danger to which we are exposed, at times of trial, is this: to *despise* the chastening of the LORD.

"My son, *despise* not thou the chastening of the LORD." "Despise it not;" *i.e.*, do not think lightly of it. It is a crisis in your life; a time

when God is speaking to you; when the earthly
cisterns are broken;—when the grave is open;—
when you wake up, perhaps, to feel that from
your home, light and happiness are gone for
ever. "All joy is darkened, the mirth of the
land is gone." It is a crisis, for good or evil.
Do not think lightly of it.

Till we have humbled ourselves, and learned
to know Jesus, we all of us, more or less, "despise the chastening of the Lord:"—and sometimes, even afterwards. We look upon the trial
as a sort of *interruption* to our active life, to be
borne as best we can, and got rid of, as soon as
possible. If it is some one else who is in sorrow,
we wonder why they do not "keep up better,"
—why they are not braver, etc. If it is ourselves,
we pity ourselves, or merely bring our *natural*
powers to bear on it. When a man has a strong
natural will, it is marvellous to see how he brings
that will—like the natural courage of some ani-
mals—to bear upon it. A man knows, for instance, that he must die, and knows that he is
not prepared for death; yet he faces it with a resolute will, and endures his sufferings even better

than many a devout Christian, because they are
not aggravated by the temptations of Satan. Marvellous courage is often shown, where there is a
strong natural will.   Or it may be a poor weak
man; and then, his courage fails, and he com-
plains, and wants every body to pity and comfort
him.   It is a mere difference of temperament.
In either case, the trial is regarded as an acci-
dent—an interruption: the chastening of the
LORD is *despised*.   The only thought is this:
"My place in the active world is empty; the
great thing is, to get well as soon as possible,
and go back to it.   These times must come, and
we must get over them as well as we can;" etc.
And so, the "interruption" over, the man goes
back to his business, or the young girl goes to
stay with friends, to drive out thought; to get rid
of the sorrow, as an unwelcome visitor !

And yet, what is it—this "chastening of the
LORD?"   It is a part of GOD's education; one of
GOD's great methods of converting or sanctifying
us; a "means of grace."   Even in trifles, we
should not lose this idea.   Our little every-day
worries are to be endured as in the sight of GOD;

not as mere accidents or interruptions; not apart
from GOD; not hiding ourselves from Him
"among the trees of the garden." "Despise
not thou the chastening of the LORD."

Our TEMPTATION, then, is to *despise* GOD's
chastening; to try to bear it *outside* of GOD. How
shall we find the REMEDY.

We must fix our eyes on the Person of our
Blessed LORD. "Consider HIM." Observe how,
in all His trials,—in His greatest Agony, He
never lost sight of this fact;—it was the Will of
GOD. He never permitted Himself to do what
we are so apt to do,—to look at secondary causes;
to eliminate the idea of GOD, as the First Cause.
Calmly He looked at His judge. "Thou could-
est have no power at all against Me, except it
were given thee from above."—"The cup which
My FATHER hath given Me, shall I not drink
it?"—"Thinkest thou that I can not now pray
to My FATHER, and He shall presently give Me
more than twelve legions of angels? But how
then shall the Scripture be fulfilled, that thus it
must be?"

There is a mighty power, a mighty antidote

against despising the chastening of the LORD, in simply gazing on that Crucified One.   Beneath, is the jeering crowd; there He hangs, alone; His little band of disciples, gone; and the Virgin Mother, and St. John.   He is left alone.   What is the thought specially present to His mind? My FATHER has given Me this Cup.   My FATHER has bound me to this Cross.   While all below are scoffing, He, in the highest part of His Being, is calmly dealing with the Unseen.   He is · suffering as in the sight of GOD; as in the Presence of the Invisible FATHER.   "My GOD, my GOD, why hast Thou forsaken Me?" What means this new dealing with Thy SON? "FATHER, into Thy Hands I commend My Spirit."

We have found the REMEDY:—to draw in power from that aspect of the Passion of JESUS CHRIST, in which we regard Him as suffering in the Presence of the Eternal and Invisible FATHER.

The Second Danger to which we are specially exposed, in Suffering, is that of *fainting* under the trial. "My son, despise not thou the chastening of the LORD, nor *faint* when thou art rebuked of Him."

As the stricken deer flees before its pursuers, to hide itself among the trees and die, so the wounded heart wishes to be alone; away from the ordinary calls of life, free from demands on its sympathy. "I have enough to bear, of my own; why should I pity others? My own cross is the heaviest; my own life, the most lonely." Selfishness becomes almost inevitable.

This temptation to think of Self comes to all; even to the holiest. And thus, Love is choked and hindered. We grow weary and faint in our minds. We are tempted to become hard:—hard to others, and sometimes, even to GOD our FATHER! "Why does GOD give me so much trial, —such bodily weakness, or mental suffering and depression?" The burden does indeed seem heavy! Like Job, we are tempted to "curse GOD and die"; like David, to say: "I have cleansed my heart in vain." What profit is there in religion? Why am I so tried, while others are spared? Why is there no golden harvest for me? Why are those whom I love, not yet turned to God?

Disappointment, trial, and sorrow, if not sanctified, make men *hard.* It is often observed that, in prosperity, people are so pleasant! In adversity, there is a temptation to sink down into a cold, stolid, unloving frame of mind; absorbed in self; for selfishness is the *natural* effect of trial and sorrow.

But remember, you will never *realize* this—you will never find out that you are selfish in sorrow, till you have humbled yourself under the mighty Hand of God. For "comfort," in the inner life, as well as in the outer life, is our *natural* idea. And so, we "think it strange," when any fiery trial comes to us; we faint, when we are "rebuked of Him."

What is the ANTIDOTE to this evil?

Gaze, day by day, on that unselfish Life of His,—the Man of Sorrows! "Consider HIM" (Heb. xii. 3). Surely there was enough to occupy HIM, in His own sorrows? Yet see Him, —though feeling it all as keenly as any of *us* would have felt it,—stopping on the way to Je-

rusalem, to help that blind man: a mere beggar;
perhaps, we might have thought, only an impostor! See Him, waiting for Bartimæus, listening
to his petition, opening his eyes.

Think of Him, in Gethsemane, watching His
opportunity, before the multitude came up, to
make a gentle appeal to Judas. "Friend, wherefore art thou come?" Even to Judas, in the
midst of that agony unspeakable! (Ps. lv. 12–14.)
Even to Judas, who betrayed Him!

"Follow to the Judgment-Hall." Think of
His LOVE unutterable, in all the cold wretchedness of that morning! Watch Him, weary, exhausted, after being up all night, without food
or rest, among His persecutors. And remember,
He was "Very Man." Surely, He had enough
to bear? Yet, there was time to think of Peter,
even there! "The LORD turned, and looked
upon Peter" (St. Luke xxii. 61).

There was time, on the way to Calvary, to
think of the poor women of Jerusalem. "Weep
not for Me!" There was time, even with the
nails in His Hands, to pray for those who crucified Him; to speak to the thief on the Cross be-

side Him; to comfort and save that penitent thief.
There was time to think of the Virgin-Mother
and St. John, to whom those last three hours,
and the cry, "My GOD, my GOD, why hast Thou
forsaken Me?" would have been more than they
could bear. There was time to speak those
words: "Behold thy Mother," "Behold thy
son"; so that the Virgin and St. John were
gone from the Cross, before those last three
hours of darkness came on.

We follow this JESUS of Nazareth; we think
of Him as Very Man; we try to analyze the elements of His Suffering, bodily, mental, spiritual.
And we see Self dead, buried;—and JESUS, with
His Heart free for others, not separating Himself
from His brethren, but bearing their burdens,
afflicted in all their afflictions; ready to use the
power of His Godhead to save *them*, though for
Himself no legion of angels was invoked.

And we learn this: There is a power in the
Passion of JESUS; a power which the HOLY
GHOST is able to bring down,—observe this:—*a
power which the* HOLY GHOST *is able and willing
to bring down*—into each poor fainting, suffering

soul, as it gazes on the unselfish Passion of JESUS.

"He giveth power to the faint, and to them that have no might He increaseth strength. Even the youths shall faint and be weary;—but they that wait upon the LORD shall renew their strength; they shall run, and not be weary; they shall walk, and *not faint*" (Is. xl. 29–31).

"Consider Him that endured such contradiction of sinners against Himself, lest ye be wearied and faint in your minds". (Heb. xii. 3).

We begin the Christian life so brightly, so earnestly; willing to sacrifice health, character, every thing. It may be hard; but it is a bright life. When first we are brought to CHRIST, we make up our minds, that in our own homes they shall see how happy our religion makes us.

But presently, dark days come; temptations in the wilderness; times when prayer seems a mockery. And then, as the iron enters into the soul, deeper and deeper, there is danger of "fainting"; of giving it all up; of saying: "It is no use, for me; my case is peculiar; there is so much opposition, etc. I can not be what I hoped to be." Our ideal is crushed. We grow weary and faint; as, on an Eastern journey, the brightness of morning is succeeded by the depression of noon. Many an earnest soul, that has lived for GOD, worked for GOD, is ready to die for GOD,—*faints;* does not lose its spiritual life, but ceases to be a power for good. The battle is *too* hard !

O my brother, my sister, listen ! Remember, that although JESUS CHRIST is Very Man, yet He is also "Very GOD"; "Light of Light"; "Equal to the FATHER"; "the mighty GOD" (Is. ix. 6). And this His Godhead has been brought down from Heaven to earth, by the Mystery of the Incarnation.

You may be tempted, on the one hand, to "*despise* the chastening of the LORD;" and thus lose the blessing intended. Or you may be tempted to "*faint* when rebuked of Him;" you may kneel at the Holy Table, having *almost* made up your mind that the battle is *too* hard; that the ideal of Christian life is not possible, for you.

But never let Satan blind you to this fact: that

HE Whom you follow, even JESUS, is Very GOD, as well as Very Man;—that *the Power of the Passion can be poured into your soul, by* GOD *the* HOLY GHOST.

Is this language too strong? But what does the inspired Apostle say? (Eph. iii. 14-21.) What was his prayer for each of his people at Ephesus? That they 'might be just saved;— that they might not fall back into old sins?

No! More than this! He prayed that all the fulness of the Godhead might be poured into those weak vessels of humanity, so that they might become *almighty*, through the Divine power poured into them! And then,—as if it seemed too much to ask, for these poor tempted Ephesians, that such as these might be "filled with all the fulness of GOD,"—the HOLY SPIRIT reminded him of the blessed fact: "HE is able," etc.; and so the chapter ends with an ascription of glory "unto Him, Who is able to do exceeding abundantly above all that we ask or think."

It would seem a blessed fruit of this Holy Week, if our LORD JESUS CHRIST promised, by the power of His Godhead, to give us *all that we asked.* But He is "able to do exceeding abundantly *above* all that we ask," or even "think!" He Who died for us, as in this Holy Week, is "Very God!" And He longs to fill each of your hearts, at this holy time, with "all the fulness of God."

Gaze on your suffering LORD! Gaze on Him, with humble prayer; look up to Him, even if you find no words. And the prayers offered throughout Christendom at this time shall be answered for you; and you shall learn, so as you have never learned before, THE POWER OF THE PASSION OF JESUS; applied, as you will, to the life of Action, or to the life of Suffering.

Good Friday.

MY object, to-day, is to help you to think for yourselves; to help you to see how each of you, with your individual soul, may draw near to Him Who died for you, as on this day.

If any of you, through bodily or spiritual weakness, are unable to think, or to follow the teaching given, do not be disheartened. "Be still;" humbling yourselves in silence, or almost in silence, before GOD. Say to Him: "O LORD, Thy Hands were pierced for me! Thou didst say: My GOD, My GOD, why hast Thou forsaken Me? Have mercy on me!" Or take the Psalms and the Gospel for the day, and turn them into prayer. So will you find words enough, and far more than enough; and thoughts will be given you by the HOLY SPIRIT, according to your need.

Even for those who are able to enter more into it, I do not wish to offer new thoughts. For the object of this quiet hour is that, in the solemn stillness, old thoughts and old words may come back to the heart, by the power of the HOLY GHOST.

Do not be in a worry, a spiritual worry, as if everything depended on this Good Friday! There is a nervous, fidgetty spirit, even in religion, which blinds us to the fact that "JESUS CHRIST" is "the Same yesterday, and to-day, and forever;" the Same, before Good Friday, and on Good Friday, and after Good Friday. Abiding in Him, the power of the Cross is not limited to these three hours! But, at the same time, honor GOD by expecting a blessing.

Remember, you are still "in the body" (II Cor. v. 4, 6). Stay no longer than you have strength to stay. Go no longer without food than you are able. "Your FATHER knoweth that ye have need of these things." "He remembereth that we are but dust." Use your Christian freedom wisely (St. Luke xii. 30; Ps. ciii. 14; St. Mark viii. 1–3; Heb. iv. 15).

And then, expect a blessing, to-day, of all days! For to-day, we feel that the blessed Angels must be especially watching, longing to rejoice over our growth in grace. To-day, we feel that the Heavenly Bridegroom must be looking, with love unspeakable, on that Bride, the Church, whom He purchased with His own Blood (Acts xx. 28). Therefore, expect a blessing; ask the HOLY SPIRIT to give to each of us the blessing which each needs.

Lay hold of this thought. The HOLY GHOST is a Living Person, GOD's special Gift to the Church of CHRIST; Whose office it is, to take of the things of CHRIST, and show them to us, — to bring to our remembrance all things that JESUS spoke, and JESUS did. And therefore, as a Living Person, He is able to give what we ask; — as able to put thoughts and feelings into our hearts, as *we* are to put any thing into another's hands. And then, ask Him to put into our hearts, consciously, or unconsciously, — to be realized to-day, or some other day, as He sees best, — that special thought or aspect of our

LORD's Passion which He sees to be needful for each of us individually.

[Here let us pause, and say the "Veni Creator," together on our knees: "Come, Holy Ghost, our souls inspire."]

And now, remembering that we have a Living Guide and Help in the Blessed SPIRIT, let me suggest to you three different ways, any or all of which will be useful to you to-day, of meditating on the Sufferings of our LORD:—three aspects of our LORD's Passion.

I. We might spend some time, first, in thinking of the great Love of our LORD *to those who injured Him.*

Think of His Love to Malchus: to those who crucified Him; above all, to St. Peter. Quietly try to think of St. Peter, after he had denied our LORD. See Him, forgetting His own suffering and shame, and looking upon Peter with that look of Love ! Then follow St. Peter, going out and weeping bitterly. Picture him, on the evening of that Good Friday, standing, it may be, where that Cross,—where those three Crosses,— had been fixed. Try to enter into St. Peter's heart, as he thought of that look of Love.

Come, Blessed SPIRIT of Grace and of Supplication, proceeding from the FATHER and the SON, that *we* also may look on Him Whom *we* have pierced !

O Blessed LORD, how many of us have denied Thee ! Those opportunities, lost forever ! Those years that we have lost, never to be recalled ! The times when we have denied Thee, by our cowardly silence !

Think of all this; not in a dark way, like souls in bondage, but with a sad, softened feeling: like St. Peter's, when he felt that JESUS' Love was not quenched by the cold waters of his ingratitude. Think of it; not with terror and despair, but with a purifying, holy sorrow. "O that I could bring back those lost years ! And yet,—*Thou lovest me !*"

So meditate on that Look of JESUS on St. Peter. And link with it the Words of JESUS on the Cross: "Father, forgive them, for they know not what they do." Think of the answer to

that prayer which has come to *us*, in our care-
less days !

II. To-day is a day for making *resolutions.*
Bring the force of the Passion to bear on your
besetting sins.

Most of you know pretty well your special
dangers, by this time; through your self-exami-
nations and confessions to GOD, (whether alone,
or before some one else), you have been able to
make out the weak points in your character.
Now bring the thought of the Passion to bear
on those special sins and failings.

III. *Think of the Love of the Good Shepherd to
every human soul.* "I am the Good Shepherd;
the Good Shepherd giveth His Life for the sheep.
—And other sheep I have, which are not of this
fold; them also I must bring" (St. John x.
11–16). "I, if I be lifted up from the earth,
will draw all men unto Me" (St. John xii. 32).

Look at it, in the light of that chapter which
contains our LORD's Intercession for His Church,
the same night in which He was betrayed (St.

John xvii.) Think of His Intercession on the Cross: "Father, forgive them!" Think of His words to the penitent thief. Think of the "*I thirst;*"—of its deepest meaning; our LORD'S longing that none should perish, but that all men should come to Him and be saved.

Do not let Satan darken your mind and hinder your intercessions, by perplexities as to those who have passed away, and who knew not what *you* know. The light that shone upon the Church, in those days, was so different from what we have, now! Perhaps the Love of JESUS was never made known to them, and rejected.

Think of His Love for every human soul; and then, *pray* for your own parish, for the Church, for the world. So many around us, just now, seem trembling between life and death! They seem almost withered, almost cut off; little sap left; no fruit; scarcely even *leaves!* Save them, O LORD, by Thine Agony and Bloody Sweat, by Thy Cross and Passion!

So, whether in Contrition, or Resolve, or Intercession:—whether thinking what our Past has

been, and coming to our LORD to tell Him how
sorry we are; with tears of penitence, yet so
thankful for His Love; or bracing our weak
will for the Future,—to gain more force for the
fight; or to gain fresh power in Intercession;—
we come back, and stand at the foot of the
Cross.

O the Love streaming down from that Cross!
It seems so easy, to-day, to feel that all may be
saved—all made holy;—that we shall be able
really to advance in the spiritual life! Yes,
LORD, it is true; Thou hast loved us! For us,
Thou didst endure all that night of suffering;
those hours on the Cross, hanging there so
patiently, minute by minute, in Thy Love unspeakable?

O Blessed SPIRIT, as we kneel low before the
Cross, reveal that Love to us; that we may indeed
mourn, with a happy mourning, for our sins;
that we may rise with a steadfast purpose, to renew the fight; and plead, so as we never plead-
ed yet, for those for whom that Blood was
shed!

PART II. ADDRESS AT 2.30. P. M.

We have been together, for the last hour and a half, trying to realize what the LORD JESUS CHRIST suffered for us. We have been trying to realize it, so as to make it a power in our life; in Penitence for past sin. Or we have been drawing in power from the Passion, through the HOLY GHOST, to brace ourselves for our future life. Or we have been interceding, under the Cross, in the Name of Him who died on that Cross, because He loved us; Who gave His life "a Ransom for many."

And the *result* of this past hour, and of the time which yet remains, is certain; for the HOLY GHOST loves to help us.

(1.) A deeper sorrow for sin.

(2.) A more steadfast purpose, in striving against sin.

(3.) More faith in pleading for others.

Many of us, I doubt not, though conscious of much weakness and wavering,—conscious of past failure, and certain that there will again be much failure in the future,—have said: "Lo, I come, to do Thy Will, O God!" We have made up our minds,—have we not?—that *we will not contradict the Passion, in our lives;* that we will not seek what is pleasant, and avoid what is distasteful. We have made up our minds, that, in the strength of our Lord, we will be true to Him, day by day; that, however often we fail, we will persevere.

Now, for these few minutes,—while silently waiting for that clock to strike, which tells us of our Lord's Death,—we will try to lose the thought of self, and think only of Him.

"I, if I be lifted up from the earth, will draw all men unto Me." Thou art lifted up, O Blessed One! Thou wast, as at this hour, hanging on that Cross, for us! We are looking up to Thee. Draw our hearts to Thee!

From the sixth to the ninth hour,—there is "darkness!" All is still and calm, around the Cross. The Virgin Mary is gone; St. John is gone. All is silent. We seem almost to hear the drops of Blood, falling, one by one. All is dark around.

And the human Soul of our LORD is enveloped in a yet deeper darkness;—a darkness into which we are powerless to penetrate. Physical exhaustion; the unutterable sense of weariness; want of rest, all the night; want of food:—all this, producing a strain on the inner being! And in that state of weariness and exhaustion, Satan is not far off. There is darkness, in the Soul of JESUS. (O Blessed SPIRIT, guide each word! Save me from uttering one word that would be untrue or irreverent!) The thought is presented to Him of the sins of ages past; the sins of generations yet unborn. His consciousness is darkened with a sense of sin; though the sin is not His, but ours. "The LORD hath laid on Him the iniquity of us all." He "bare our sins, in His own Body, on the Tree." There was a dark consciousness of sin; and, it may be, a physical shrinking from death.

Into all this we can enter, to some extent. But just at this time, there came a yet deeper

darkness, into which we *can not* enter.   He, the
Son of God, is losing the consciousness of His
Father's Love !   Having, by voluntary abnega-
tion of Himself, through the Incarnation, be-
come "Very Man,"—conditioned, for the time,
by His Humanity;—knowing that He had a
Father, but having lost the consciousness of
His Love;—He *tasted Death !*

Bodily death was nothing, compared with this
spiritual dying.   O the darkness that was around
Thy Soul, Blessed Jesus, as at this time !   Make
it real to us !   Help us to treasuree it up, for our
times of darkness; for the days when prayer seems
a mockery, and God seems far away, and we also
cry: "My God, my God, why hast Thou forsaken me ? "

Then, the Agony was over.   St. John, with
the wondrous intuition of Love, under the guid-
ance of the Holy Ghost, tells us, that "after
this, Jesus *knowing that all things were now ac-
complished,* saith: I thirst."   There was the calm
return to the consciousness of His Father's Love.

"I thirst!"   O what a Thirst that was !   For
your soul, and for mine !   O sacred Thirst,—

that His FATHER's Will might be *fulfilled;* that all might be saved, and come to a knowledge of the Truth ! O blessed Thirst, to which we come back in days of doubt and darkness, and thank GOD for the assurance it involves:—"This is the Will of GOD, even your sanctification."

And then He said: "IT IS FINISHED !" "FATHER, INTO THY HANDS I COMMEND MY SPIRIT."

And then,—at this very hour,—at three o'clock, (the time of the Evening Sacrifice,) JESUS "bowed His Head, and gave up the ghost."

There should be no thought of Self in us, now; —no thought *for* Self. Quietly let us kneel, and think of JESUS—*crucified.*

Easter Eve.

" REST IN THE LORD." (Marginal Reading:
" Be silent to the LORD."—Ps. xxxvii. 7.)

THE worst, dear brethren, is over now, and
our LORD is laid in that quiet grave. Joseph of
Arimathæa and Nicodemus have now lost all their
cowardice, and come forward to claim His Body.
That which the Life of JESUS was powerless to ef-
fect, has been wrought in them by the Death of
JESUS on Calvary. They have looked on Him
Whom they have pierced, and " Jacob" is now
" Israel:" bold, brave, decided.

Tenderly they have taken down that Body, and
wrapped It in the linen. The poor women are
there, who had cheered Him during His Life on
earth. Mary Magdalene and the other Mary sit
down and watch where the Body of JESUS is laid
(St. Matt. xxvii. 55, 56, 61).

Mary Magdalene:—she who had been greatly

forgiven! The unpardoned soul thinks:—"What
can I *gain* from CHRIST? How much comfort
can I get out of religion? How much of the
world may I have, and yet escape hell? The unpardoned soul is always bargaining with GOD;—
making merchandise in that heart which is the
Temple of GOD. But the pardoned soul,—the
soul that feels its sin, and feels the power of the
Blood of JESUS CHRIST to cleanse it,—longs to
give *all* to CHRIST. So, Mary Magdalene is there,
watching the place where the Body of JESUS is
laid.

And in the world unseen, there is another pardoned sinner, very near JESUS CHRIST:—the penitent thief.

It must have been a strange entrance for that
soul, into Paradise! There is a picture in Isaiah
xiv., of some man of mighty intellect and power,
one who on earth had been respected and distin-
guished,—there is a picture given in that ancient
prophecy, of that great man, entering into the
world unseen; and those who dwell therein are
pictured as rising up to meet him. "Hell"—
the grave—"is moved for thee, to meet thee at

thy coming: it stirreth up the Dead for thee. All they shall speak and say unto thee: Art thou also become weak as we? Art thou become like unto us?"

Surely, again and again, that scene is witnessed in the world unseen, of which the veil is thus raised for a moment.

And in another and a very different sense, we can picture the Saints in Paradise, welcoming that happy, forgiven thief into their company. We can imagine Abraham, and all the Holy Ones, almost *startled*, if we may so speak, when they saw, entering Paradise, the man who, the day before, had been hanging as a malefactor on the cross! But *with* that soul was One, thank GOD, Who had the right of giving entrance. In that Kingdom wherein they dwell, He has the keys; He can open, and none can shut. He had claimed that thief for Himself, and had promised to him: "To-day shalt thou be with Me in 'Paradise!" And so, all that glorious Company welcomed him, because he was with JESUS.

O that this may be *our* welcome from the

Saints in Light, when this short life is over!
"Thou art become *one of us;* for thou hast
washed thy robes, and made them white in the
Blood of the Lamb!"

But we must return, and look again at the
Sepulchre.

Even on earth, we connect two thoughts,
especially, with Death:—REST, and SILENCE.
When we have watched the poor spirit struggling to escape,—when we have seen the heav-
ing breast panting for a release which seems
denied to it,—when we have watched that last
struggle,—O the Rest, as we enter the chamber
of death, and see those hands so meekly folded,
—a farewell said to earthly storms! Even to
look at a dead body, seems to calm angry pas-
sions,—to solemnize the heart even of a child!

But this is "the Body of the LORD JESUS!"
(St. Luke xxiv. 3.) And the thought that we
have carried with us through the Holy Week, is
this:—the LORD JESUS is not only Very Man, but
Very GOD; One Who can pour His Life into us,
according to our need. "The last Adam was

made a *quickening* Spirit" (1 Cor. xv. 45). We have seen how CHRIST, in the power of his GOD-HEAD, is able to take our poor weak humanity, and fill it with "all the fulness of GOD." And so, to-day, when thinking of that hardest strug-gle of all, to "*rest* in the LORD,"—to "be *still;*" —when we feel how hard it is, especially for some temperaments, we thank GOD that, for this also, there is Life laid up for us in JESUS CHRIST.

As, in the days of old, when that dead man was "cast into the sepulchre of Elisha," and "touched the bones of Elisha," he lived (2 Kings xiii 21), so now, on this quiet Easter Eve, when we draw near to the Sepulchre in which JESUS is laid, and touch that dead Body, as it were, life shall flow into us:—the life of Silence, and of Rest.

As years roll on, and strength fades away, let us kneel down, every Friday, and think of the Precious Blood shed for us; and every Saturday, let us kneel at His Sepulchre, and remind our-selves of death,—of the words that will soon be said over us: "Ashes to ashes, dust to dust." And thus, with the quiet preparation of that Sat-urday—so different from the bustling Saturday

of the world!—let us end the week with JESUS;
so that the Easter morning of every Sunday, with
its Holy Communion, may be the foretaste of
the great Resurrection of all whom we have
loved on earth. "For if we believe that JESUS
died, and rose again, even so them also which
sleep in JESUS will GOD bring with Him."

We lose much, by not learning the spirit of
Simeon and Anna,—the spirit of quiet waiting,
in this hurrying life!

I. From the Passion of CHRIST, then, we can
draw power for the life of Silence.

Sometimes, nothing is so hard as to be silent.
It costs a long effort, a hard struggle. We think
we have formed the habit; and then, something
comes to try us, and we seem to have lost it all!

How little silence there is! What strife of
tongues! Every one railing, protesting, argu-
ing! The man of science, advancing his crude
theories; the religious man answering him, with
theories no less crude; High Church against Low
Church; Low Church against High Church;
brother against brother; class against class:—

every one laying down the law, as if GOD had given to each a revelation peculiar to himself! In private life, too; the sister hindering the spiritual life of her sister; parents crushing the spiritual life out of their children; children grieving their parents with impatient answers, insubordination, etc.; even husband and wife, hindering one another's prayers!

How is it all to be prevented? Fight against it with fleshly weapons, and you only increase the evil.

Watch JESUS, in this quiet hour! Watch Him, silent before Pilate and Herod, "so that Pilate marvelled." Watch Him, "led as a lamb to the slaughter;" dumb "as a sheep before her shearers." Watch Him, in His silence. And then, say to Him: "LORD, I have tried to be silent; I have failed. But Thou art the Living Head, and I am a member of Thy Mystical Body. Pour Thy silent Life into my feverish, restless spirit! LORD, I *will* trust Thee! If I have to wait till I die, before I have learnt to be silent, still I will trust Thee. Pour Thy silent life into my heart!"

But this thought needs to be guarded. Those who have studied the art of aggravating others, know that a word would sometimes hurt far less, than a dogged, aggrieved, determined silence. If we make up our minds to be *always* silent, for fear of increasing the strife of tongues, we shall fail on the other side. If we make up our minds that we will *never* speak of GOD, because certain persons become too familiar, irreverent, "canting," in telling you what GOD has done for their souls, then we dishonor GOD, we rob our brethren, and we drive people to Dissent.

More than this. If, because our ideal is not realized in Christian intercourse,—if, because we long to be hidden from the strife of tongues, we resolve to be *always* silent, then, we hide our talent in a napkin; we lose the opportunity that was given us by GOD; we are silent, but we are not "silent *to the Lord.*" This therefore must be corrected, in the same way as the other side,—by again gazing on the Character and Life of our LORD.

There was a time, during the Passion, when His enemies were perfectly infuriated with Him

for His silence. I have seen a man half mad-
dened, because his wife would not curse him in
return, but only lifted up her heart to God, silently. And thus it was, when He gave His
back to the smiters, and His cheeks to them that
plucked off the hair (Is. l. 6).

But when He saw that silence would do harm,
then, Jesus spoke. So humbly !   "If I have
spoken evil; bear witness of the evil."   And this
was "God manifest in the flesh !"   O the Hu-
mility of Jesus !   How it draws us to Him, when
we think that this is He Who is to be our Judge,
—He who is our Guide through life; this tender,
compassionate Jesus, Who thus humbled Himself even to the rough "officer" who struck Him
with the palms of his hands !

So again, when the High Priest adjured Him
by the Living God to tell him if He was the
Christ, silence was broken, and Jesus spoke.

When opportunity came to do good by speaking, when silence would have been dishonor to
God, then, Jesus did not hold back;—even
though it must be to tell of the "fire that is
not quenched;"—even though it must be to

say:—"Ye serpents, ye generation of vipers, how can ye escape the damnation of Hell?" He Who has told us, that when a man sins against us, we are to watch our opportunity, and tell him of the sin, lest that sin, unforgiven, should ruin his soul,—He Himself, when evil weighed on the people, spoke the words which the FATHER had given into His keeping, and told them of their sins.

Though His lips might quiver, and His voice falter, and His eyes fill with tears, as He uttered the doom on the City that *would* not be saved, yet, when it was to speak for His FATHER,—to do His "FATHER's business,"—then, calmly and tenderly, but most truly, JESUS spoke.

And now we come, with those women, and sit over against the Sepulchre; and we think of that silent Saviour, and we say: "LORD, how can I ever know the right time to speak, and to be silent? How can I know whether I am silent *to Thee*, O LORD, or only *to myself?* Pour Thy grace into my heart! Supply all my need, out of Thy fulness; for Thou art the Head of the

Body. Thou art made unto us Wisdom. Thou
canst give to me what I can never find for myself. LORD, I shall fail, even to the end; but to
the end I will trust Thee! They that know Thy
Name shall put their trust in Thee; for thou,
LORD, hast *never* failed them that seek Thee."

And my brother, He will never fail thee! You
may think that you have gained nothing of the
wisdom of Silence; but those who watch you
narrowly will tell a different story. They will
tell us that it is not what it was. The old temper does still break out, sometimes, but it is not
what it used to be. Your soul has been baptized into the Silence of JESUS.

II. The Life of REST. These two ideas are so
linked,—Silence and Rest,—that there is no need
to dwell at length upon the thought of Rest.
It is only a different translation of the same
word.

"Rest?"—Some of you will answer; "never,
on this side of the grave, for *me!* Nothing for
me, but worry, disappointment, dissatisfaction,
schemes failing;—all I do, ending in failure!

Early do I rise, and late take rest. GOD can not count *me* as one of 'His Beloved,' to whom He giveth sleep. It is little Rest that *I* have ! "

Another says: How am I to find Rest, among the conflict of *opinions ?* You teach one thing; another man, equally good, teaches something different. What am I to believe? What is Truth? Where shall I find Rest, for my mind? "O that I had wings like a dove, for then would I flee away, and be at rest ! "

Or you are perplexed, with *spiritual* perplexity, "How much, in my trials, is from my own fault? How much is of GOD's appointing? I can bear any thing, if it is 'the cup which my FATHER hath given me;' I can bear any thing, if it is to please HIM. But—I know my motives are not quite perfect; I know that I was not quite true, at the beginning. How far has this marred the whole? They must be clean, who bear the vessels of the LORD. All this discipline, which you tell me is sent in Love, to link me with JESUS, is not that, to me; it is a punishment. God is leaving me to myself, because I have sinned."

O the mingling of motives, in our hearts !

"Who can understand his errors?" How are we tied and bound with the chains of our sins!

Sometimes, as the only comfort that the poor soul is capable of receiving just then, the LORD JESUS bids us look into His Sepulchre, and see Him laid there, all suffering over; His Body resting so calmly, after all that agony; His Spirit at rest, among the spirits in Paradise! Sometimes, the only comfort which a soul can receive is this:—It will not last for ever! Perhaps, this year,—perhaps, this very night,—I shall be with CHRIST in Paradise!

> "A few more toils, a few more tears,
> And we shall weep no more."

But this is not enough—to know that the battle will be over, some day. We want something that will give us Rest, now, even amid all the tossing to and fro; like the depths of the ocean, calm beneath all outer suffering. How shall we gain this inward Rest?

To you, dear people, who have been following me through the Week's teaching, the answer is easy. By looking at our LORD, and asking Him to pour His Rest into our souls.

"O rest *in the Lord!*" Hide in the Cleft of the Rock. JESUS CHRIST has been made a "Hiding-Place from the wind," for you and me; the Rock of Ages.

> "Rock of Ages, cleft for me,
> Let me hide myself in Thee."

However weary and heavy-laden we may be, in body, soul, or spirit; however perplexed with the contradictory teaching of the day; yet, if we know JESUS CHRIST as a Living Person,—if we know that we have a Friend Who is thinking of us in Heaven, we may feel sure that He will give us sufficient light to guide us to the Crystal Sea, where every question will be solved, every difficulty removed. And so we can rest, because sure of the PERSON in Whom we trust. He knows all, and He loves us: not because we are good, but because He, the Loving One, *chooses* to love us, and came to seek and to save the lost.

The best way to drive away Satan, when we are

harassed and perplexed, is to say to JESUS CHRIST: "LORD, Thou knowest all things. Thou knowest how wicked I am. Thou knowest my motives, bad and good. Thou knowest all the sins that I have confessed to Thee again and again. But it would be a still greater sin, to doubt Thy LOVE!"

And as we kneel there, in our penitence and trust, He Who is so tender and so comforting, never breaking the bruised reed, will come to us, many a time, and whisper to us words like these: "Be not faithless, but believing! Only abide in Me! I died on that Cross, for thee; I was buried, I rose again, for thee; I am pleading in Heaven, for thee. When thou liest there, so stricken,—unable to feel, to love, to trust,—the great High Priest is ever presenting His finished Sacrifice for thee; ever pleading for thee, behind the Veil, by that Agony and Bloody Sweat, that Cross and Passion."

But I should be mocking you, dear people, if I ended here. IS YOUR HEART YIELDED TO CHRIST? I should be an unfaithful Pastor, if I allowed you

to go away, dreaming of rest and peace, if you
will not take His yoke upon you; if you will not
kneel down and acknowledge that you are lost,
and bear the travail-pain through which God
brings His children,—gradually or suddenly,—
out of the darkness of a merely nominal religion,
into conscious light and liberty; if, in plain words,
you have never come to your Saviour, and found
"Rest unto your souls;"—the "Rest" of a realized Forgiveness,—of "Pardon and Peace."

God forbid that I should say you can not be
saved, without this *conscious* pardon; but I am
quite sure that you lose half the brightness and
the power of your Christian life. It is not of
"conversion" (St. Matt. xviii. 3) that I am now
speaking to you, who have been kneeling with
me during this Holy Week. I want you to have
the true Easter joy. Before the Monday and
Tuesday, with their special teaching, I want you
to have passed through this first stage;—to have
been consciously purged from past sins; to know
the blessedness of him whose unrighteousness is
forgiven, and whose sin is covered. I want you
to come to the Cross of Jesus Christ, and let

your burden fall into the Sepulchre. It is "hard by" the Cross;—very near!

Keep your eye on the Cross; and if you can not get clear, tell me, and let me help you.

Come, and have Rest! Not the Rest of idleness, but Rest from the burden of unforgiven sin; Rest from the strife of tongues;—the problem solved: "Is God for us, or against us?"—the heart "set at liberty" (Ps. cxix. 32); free to live, and, if need be, to die, for the Lord Who lived and died for you.

Dear people, can there be a doubt, this Holy Week, if He loves you? Has not Jesus Christ been evidently set forth, crucified among you?. Have you not *seen* His Love;—His tears, even over those who rejected Him? And can you doubt if He loves you, that have *not* rejected Him?

Kneel down, and tell your sins to your God. Act on the teaching which you have so often heard here. "Take with you words, and turn to the Lord" (Hosea xiv. 2). Come to Him, and say:—

"Just as I am, without one plea,
But that Thy Blood was shed for me
And that Thou bidst me come to Thee,
O Lamb of God, I come!"

Do not put it off! For there is a mighty spiritual current, at this time, flowing through Christendom: prayer is ascending, day and night; and hearts are softened by hearing of the Sufferings of Jesus; and nations are "born in a day!" Every Pastor will tell you how astonished he has been at the rapidity with which, at such times, souls realize their sin, and their pardon. "I, if I be lifted up from the earth, will draw all men unto Me." There is an Almighty Power working with us:—the Power of the Holy Ghost. The Cross was not more fixed on Calvary, than it is fixed in the midst of us now, by the Holy Ghost. "He shall testify of Me."

For thee,—whoever thou art, who believest in Jesus Christ, there is Rest, a blessed Rest, in Him: for *thy* sin was buried in that Sepulchre.

"O rest in the Lord!" Do not remain like this church on Easter Eve, with half the trappings of Lent still left, while Easter decorations have begun! Let yours be the full Easter joy, even though you wrestle all night for it:—the joy of being able to say: "Thanks be to God, Who hath given me the victory:—not because I am good, but because CHRIST died for me, and rose again, and ever liveth to make intercession for me."

Easter Day.

"WORTHY IS THE LAMB THAT WAS SLAIN, TO RE-
CEIVE POWER, AND RICHES, AND WISDOM, AND STRENGTH,
AND HONOR, AND GLORY, AND BLESSING."—(Rev. v. 12.)

AMONG the many blessings which we enjoy in
that part of CHRIST's Church to which we belong,
few are greater than the holy restraint which takes
us away from the exclusive contemplation of any
one truth—any *one* side of the spiritual life, or
of GOD's Revelation, — because the experience
of ages has shown that the exaggerated contemplation of that one truth, day by day, is hurtful
to spiritual development.

For nearly forty days, with more or less
earnestness, we have been looking into our
own hearts; examining ourselves, as in the Presence of the Judge before Whom we may at any
moment be called to appear. Some of you, I
doubt not, have analyzed your own hearts,
searched into the secret springs of your activity,

traced your besetting sin to its source, till you
are weary of your sin, weary of repenting of it,
weary of your own selves.   The more we look
at ourselves, the more we feel: "In me, that is,
in my flesh, dwelleth *no* good thing." The .
more we bring the light of the world unseen to
bear upon our hearts and lives, the more is the
cry wrung out from our inmost being: "GOD be
merciful to me, a sinner!"

And so, when the strain was becoming more
than we could bear, the Church, a fortnight ago,
began to lead us away from ourselves, away from
the *subjective* side of Christianity, to gaze on Him
Who is "lifted up," in the midst of us, this Holy
Week, that by the power of His Passion He may
draw to Himself all the best affections of a redeemed humanity.   Weary of self, we are thankful, in Holy Week and Easter-tide, to take up
the Eucharistic Hymn,—that grand old strain in
the Holy Communion Office, by which martyrs
have been nerved to die, singing praise to GOD
Incarnate.   Tired of ourselves,—tired of our
sins, our unreality, our wavering resolutions,
our halting resolves, our half-hearted prayers,

our barren meditations, our lifeless Communions, we take up the old strain, and say: "Thou only art holy; Thou only art the LORD, most high in the Glory of GOD the Father." We are weak, helpless, sinful. But in THEE, we appear before GOD. In THEE, we have died, we have risen again, we stand accepted before the Eternal One; for Thou art worthy; Thou hast redeemed us by Thy Blood; we are complete, in Thee.

This was precisely the condition of the spiritual consciousness of the Apostle, when the vision of my text was vouchsafed to him. An exile for the sake of CHRIST, he had been brought face to face with the concentrated power of the world, the flesh, and the Devil. He had had to confront all that the enemy could do, to stamp out the "sect" of the Nazarenes. He had seen every thing done that could be done, to obliterate their name from the page of history. He had seen the streets of the city filled with the blood of the martyrs—his own friends. He had seen men whom he had personally known,—men who had seemed ready to live and to die for the

sake of CHRIST—succumb to the power of the
world, the flesh, and the Devil. He had seen
heresy spring up in the Garden of the LORD.
And he himself had stood firm as a rock with
the waves beating on it; firm, on the side of the
Crucified.

What was his reward? No flaming sword was
sent by God to deliver him; no miracle wrought
to save him! Events were allowed to take their
natural course. The world was too strong for
the poor follower of CHRIST. He was driven
from home and friends, from the Church over
which he had watched, from the souls converted
by his means, or still trembling in the balance.
He was exiled, deserted; away from all other
Christians, away from those whom he loved as
his own soul.

And so, he was alone, on that Sunday, in the
Isle of Patmos; without friends to cheer him;
without even one, to whom he could open his
heart,—one, whose hand he could clasp, and
say: " *We* believe, both of us, in JESUS of Nazareth, do we not? It is *not* a delusion! JESUS is
the LORD, though all the world be against Him!"

Can we wonder,—we that know what the Devil is, and the awful reality of his temptations, burnt into the inmost heart,—if the Devil took advantage of all this, and tempted him to doubt? Perhaps, he had after all been mistaken! Perhaps, he had been too enthusiastic: perhaps, he had stood out too boldly against the world to which he was opposed; etc. He was very lonely, very desolate; with that loving human heart of his, craving as it did, for human sympathy.

And so, on this holy day, GOD looked upon him, in His tender Love. He sits as a Refiner, watching lest the fire should be heated beyond what we can bear; allowing it only to burn sufficiently to burn out the dross, that His own glorious Image may be seen. Just at that moment, when the fire was becoming too hot for his human nature, the thin cloud which separates us from the world unseen was gently uplifted, and St. John was allowed to look through, and to see what actually was happening in the great world beyond, while he was there on that lonely island. He was allowed to look through the open door, and see the great invisible world by which we are always surrounded.

.Try to realize St. John's position, as if it were your own. Weary of himself, disheartened with failure, almost tempted to doubt if the battle was worth fighting at all! Just then, the veil was uplifted, and he saw the great universe of God; not as it appears to us, looking from a distance, but as it really is; as it appears to God.

There is not time to enter into details. Only a few words can now be given, to enable you to enter into the teaching of that vision of Patmos, with its uplifting power.

He saw, in the centre, "a Lamb as it had been slain;" alive, yet bearing the marks of death;—even as on this Easter morning CHRIST appeared to the disciples, when He convinced the doubting ones, and showed them the marks of the nails, and of the Roman spear, saying: "Behold My Hands and My Feet, that it is I Myself."

The "Seven Horns" are the symbol of Almighty Power.

"The Mighty God!" "The LORD, which is,

and which was, and which is to come; the Almighty!" King over all! Almighty, to condemn,—though I do not like to use the word, on Easter Day; Almighty, to comfort and to strengthen; Almighty, to save (Rev. i. 8; St. Matt. xxviii. 18; Is. lxiii. 1). It was the symbol of the LORD Omnipotent, the Alpha and Omega, the Centre of Humanity; that Centre to which, sooner or later, all who are in harmony with the Mind of GOD must gravitate.

"The seven Eyes are the Seven Spirits of GOD," sent forth to guide and comfort and strengthen all the members of His Body.

And now, as the Apostle gazes, the solemn Service of the universe commences. A word of explanation is needed here that you may be able to enter into its meaning.

In this book of Revelation, there is always the principle of *representation*. You remember the "Thanksgiving Day" for the recovery of the Prince of Wales? The whole nation could not be there, in St. Paul's Cathedral; but Representatives were sent from various bodies,—from the

Army, the Navy, Parliament, etc.; so that although only a limited number could be actually present, yet all the members of those bodies throughout the whole world felt that they were being represented. All of us Clergy, for instance, though absent, felt that we were there, represented by those of the Clergy who were present.

This is the principle throughout the Book of Revelation; which reveals to us what is going on *now*, as seen by GOD, and taken part in by holy Angels, in the world unseen. Keeping this principle in mind, you will be able to follow the grand Service that is even *now* going on.

"Behold, a Door opened in Heaven!" Enter! Listen! What are the four Representatives on which GOD's Eye is resting?

(1.) Creation falls down; represented by "the four Beasts." All Creation sings the praise of GOD. "All the world doth worship Thee, the FATHER everlasting" (Ps. xix., cxlviii., etc.).

(2.) The Church; here represented by "the four and twenty Elders." (Remember, *you and I* are represented.)—What is "the new song" that they are singing? The same in which your voice and mine are even now uplifted: "Thou art worthy! For Thou wast slain, and hast redeemed us to God by Thy Blood!"

(3.) Then come the Angels; round about the Throne, and Creation, and the Church. These Angels and Archangels can not say: "Thou hast *redeemed* us by Thy Blood;" they are not saved by Christ, because they were never lost: but they also cry: "Worthy is the Lamb that was slain!"

(4.) And then comes that vague and shadowy realm, of which we are powerless to conceive: "Every creature in Heaven, and on the earth, and under the earth, and in the sea," takes up the chorus of praise and blessing.

And then Creation says: *"Amen."* O what a different "Amen" from that which we hear, from the voices of a few poor little boys, in many churches! In the days of the Early Church, the "Amens" heard by the heathen in the market-place, *converted* men!

And then the Church remembering her trials past,—remembering how often she had been almost tempted to give up in despair, can not speak, but falls down in silent reverence, and worships "HIM that liveth forever and ever."

O glorious Service! We may perhaps understand something of it, if we meditate over it quietly, with *prayer*.

Now, dear brethren, do not you see what a blessing such a revelation must have been to St. John? He had been looking at his own little circle, till he was so absorbed in his own troubles and trials, that he perhaps made self the centre of the universe! And then GOD opened his eyes, and showed him that great universe, of which he was only a member, and of which JESUS CHRIST was the Centre. As a man, coming from some lonely place, finds a *rest* in busy London, and loses the sense of his own petty cares, as he watches the full tide of the great city, and feels the common brotherhood of men, so was it with St. John in Patmos. GOD saw that His servant was desolate; and therefore He lifted the Veil, and showed him the great universe beyond, and CHRIST the Centre of it all.

It was as though He had said to St. John:
"Behold ! Creation, and the ransomed ones, and
all the holy Angels, and even worlds, of which
you have never heard:—before Whom do they
fall down and worship? The Lamb ! The very
LORD for Whom you are suffering ! HE is worthy, for Whom you are exiled; for Whom you
have borne all this trial, and doubt and sorrow,
—all the strugglings of your lower nature; for
Whom you have become the very scorn of men,
and the outcast of the people. HE is worthy to
be the Centre of the universe.

And *you belong to Him!* This life is but a
short parenthesis in Eternity; what matter to
you, a few short years of suffering ! You belong
to the King of Kings, and LORD of Lords. You
have learned to know Him; His Word is pledged,
never to forsake you. You knew Him in early
life, as "the Carpenter's Son," Who won your
heart by the shores of Galilee. You remember
how He had been tempted, those forty days, in
the wilderness; how the Devil had been powerless to drag Him away from His allegiance to
His Father. You remember those three years

spent with Him, when He went about doing good. You remember Him, in that Holy Week, when all were against Him; how He stood there, calm and silent, ready to be "led like a sheep to the slaughter," dumb before His shearers; ready for the Agony of Gethsemane, and the Cross of Calvary. You saw Him, with the Devil, the world, and the flesh, all ranged against Him; you stood by His Cross; you went to His Sepulchre. You were with Him after He rose again; you saw Him ascend into Heaven; you watched Him pass through the thin veil that separates this world from the world unseen, till the cloud had received Him out of your sight.—Lift up your heart! See what He is now! Centre of the Universe; Head of the Church; Alpha and Omega; the First and the Last! And you belong to Him; you are linked with Him; you are a member of His Body! Be strong and of a good courage; for the CHRIST to Whom you belong is worthy to receive all the strength of your life,—the sacrifice of your entire being.

The position which St. John occupied is the position that we also occupy. We are weak, helpless, tempted; we may have sinned, this very morning; but—unless by wilful rejection, we have cut ourselves off—we "belong to CHRIST" (St. Mark ix. 41). We have been "baptized into CHRIST." We have believed in Him. We have "put on CHRIST" (Gal. iii. 27). We are linked with Him. "We are members of His Body" (Eph. v. 30). His victories are ours.

As the little boy, when he goes to school, becomes proud of the honors gained by his school, so may the poorest and weakest and most tempted among us glory in the victories of our LORD. "Thanks be to GOD, which always causeth us to triumph IN CHRIST" (2 Cor. ii. 14). "GOD hath raised us up together, and made us sit together in Heavenly Places, in CHRIST JESUS" (Eph. ii. 6). As truly as the penitent thief was with Him in Paradise, so are we—*i.e.*, the highest part of our being—with CHRIST, already. Study this subject in the Bible, especially in the Epistle to the Ephesians. The spirit is already with CHRIST; and we are trying to uplift the mortal body, that it may be prepared to dwell with CHRIST also.

Poor tempted soul! You ask: "How can I go that long journey, and lose the privileges of Holy Communion, etc.;—I, so weak as I am? How can I fight my lonely battle? How can I help others, when so little able to live near Him myself; never making progress; always falling back?"

O my brother, remember that thou art linked with the Centre of the Universe! Thou art a member of CHRIST; and He is the Omnipotent GOD. That heart of thine, however weak and tempted, has only to be yielded to Him, to be "filled with all the fulness of GOD." When you can not stand alone, CHRIST, linked with you, will hold you up. When *you* can not fight against the temptation, CHRIST, linked with you, will fight the battle for you. When *you* can not teach others, CHRIST, linked with you, will give you the words that you need. When you are afraid to stand up and say that you are changed, and that you mean henceforth to live a new life, CHRIST will stand up with you and for you.

CHRIST for you, CHRIST with you, CHRIST in you, will conquer. "Nay, in all these things we are more than conquerors, through Him that loved us" (2 Tim. iv. 17; Rom. viii. 34–39).

Be of good cheer! Whatever your temptations,—whatever your struggles with the old nature, and the world, and the Devil,—the CHRIST in you must conquer at last! As surely as HE conquered, *you* will conquer. They nailed Him to the Cross, and made the Sepulchre sure, sealing the stone, and setting a watch: but He rose again! And so, they may take you and me, and nail us to our cross,—for the Devil *can* do this, —and we may be buried as it were, for awhile, in desolation of spirit; but when CHRIST speaks the word, the strength shall flow in, from Him, and we shall come forth from that grave,—as CHRIST came forth on this Easter Day,—conquering and to conquer; to walk, God helping us, in newness of life; dead to the old self, but alive unto GOD, through JESUS CHRIST our LORD.

Is it not sad, on a day like this, with a great congregation of baptized people, not to be able, now, simply to close the book and sing the hymn of praise? But there may be some here who have wandered from God; and the Lord Jesus Christ had a special love for those who were wandering;—for the *one* lost sheep out of the hundred. As the highest intellect can condescend most to the level of the ignorant; as the greatest of men show the most kindness to little children, so our Lord Jesus Christ, who is the Centre of the Universe, cares for that one lost sheep. He showed His greatness, when on earth, by caring most for the most weak and tempted and sinful. "How think ye? If a man have a hundred sheep, and one of them be gone astray, doth he not leave the ninety and nine, and goeth into the mountains, and seeketh that which is gone astray?" Aye, He cares for that *one* of you who is saying: "I wish I felt like that! I could bear being alone, like St. John on the Isle of Patmos, if I felt that Christ loved me; but I do *not* feel it. I would rather *not* see Christ to-night; it would be no joy, to me. Some day, I hope to be ready; but I am *not* ready now."

There is a grand old hymn that we sing at Holy Communion, which would express your feeling. It begins by joining with Angels and Archangels, as if the Veil were uplifted: "Glory be to GOD on high, and in earth peace, good-will towards men. We praise Thee, we bless Thee, we worship Thee, we glorify Thee; we give thanks to Thee for Thy great glory." And then, the Church seems to have thought that perhaps some poor soul might say, "I can not feel that!" So she sinks into a sort of minor key, and says: "*O Lamb of God, that takest away the sins of the world, have mercy upon us!*" If a soul can not say "Glory," it may at least say "Mercy!" If you can not yet say: "Glory be to GOD on high," say: "O Lamb of GOD, that takest away the sins of the world, *have mercy upon me!*"

On that first Easter Day, to whom did CHRIST first appear? To Mary Magdalene, the greatest sinner. To whom was the first message sent by the Angel? To St. Peter! Not to St. John, who was near our LORD at the Cross, but to St. Peter, who cursed and swore on that Thursday night! "Go your way, tell His disciples, *and Peter*, that He goeth before you into Galilee."

And so, to-day, I speak to you, who long to believe that your sin is washed away, and that you can start afresh. To you the Easter message is sent, as to St. Peter and Mary Magdalene. In His Name I speak, and say: "Your debt is paid. You discover that debt, little by little; but He knew it all, beforehand. And He bore it all, upon the Cross. 'It is finished!' Behold the LAMB of GOD, which taketh away the sin of the world!"

Let us enable our Blessed LORD to see, this day, of the travail of His Soul;—some souls brought out of darkness into light. "Yield yourselves unto GOD." "Seek ye the LORD while He may be found:"—*now*, while the Easter bells are still ringing!

O joy beyond all earthly joy, to be allowed to stand here and say to every soul: CHRIST loves you;—CHRIST, Who is become the Centre of humanity, the Centre of all Creation; before Whom the Angels bow with ceaseless adoration, saying: "Worthy is the LAMB that was slain to receive power and riches, and wisdom, and strength, and honor, and glory, and blessing ! "

CHRIST loves you. Believe that He loves you. Look away from self, away from your own sin. A door is opened in Heaven: look through that opened door. "BEHOLD THE LAMB OF GOD, WHICH TAKETH AWAY THE SIN OF THE WORLD ! "

Monday in Easter Week.

"I WILL PRAISE GOD, BECAUSE OF HIS WORD."—(Psalm lvi. 4, Prayer-Book version.)

HAVE you ever thought what a blessing it is, that our Easter comes in spring? It would have been so difficult to enter into Easter teaching, in the dark days of November, when the heart feels cold and withered! But spring-time reminds us that GOD is good: it speaks to us of Hope and Resurrection. Observe the beautiful Lesson for to-day, in the New Lectionary. "The winter is past; the flowers appear on the earth; the time of the singing of birds is come," etc. (Song of Solomon ii. 10–17). "So also is the Resurrection of the Dead." There shall be a spring-time for the Redeemed, in the Kingdom of GOD (1 Cor. xv. 35–38, 42, 43).

Every thing about these forty days breathes of

Hope; of calm and solemn joy; even the times chosen by our LORD to reveal Himself;—the early morning on the shore; the quiet evening at Emmaus. It is like rest after conflict; the victor on the battle-field, when the battle is ended.

And this is a side of the Christian life that must not be lost sight of, if we are to go forth conquering, and to conquer. The brightness of Easter must not be lost in the shadows of Lent. The Easter half of our life must not be left out, because there is need for Lent also.

As in a Cathedral, there is first the outer part, the porch; then, as we draw nearer, the nave; and then, the chancel, in which the Holy Communion is celebrated;—so, in Lent, we were led away from the outer world, to humble ourselves, —to look at self; and then were taught, on Passion Sunday, to look away from self, at CHRIST. Then came, to many of us, a truer—because more unselfish—mourning for sin. There was rest, all Easter Eve. And now, at Easter, the process is reversed. We look at CHRIST, risen from the dead: we think of Resurrection-life; of " the power of His Resurrection;" of the incoming of the *conquering* life, through Him Who has spoiled principalities and powers.

The Resurrection-power of CHRIST, received into the soul:—this is the thought for to-day.

To-morrow, we will try reverently to look at the Heart of JESUS in the forty days after His Resurrection; and then go back to ordinary life with a new force gathered from the Passion of our LORD, to carry us over the stormy seas; stronger than ever, from the Resurrection-Words and the Resurrection-Heart of CHRIST, to "praise GOD, because of His Word."

We are spending this week as those who have, more or less, realized their position; as those who have been taught by the HOLY SPIRIT of GOD— it matters not in what order—these truths:—that we are, in ourselves, *lost;* but that, in CHRIST, we are *saved.* Half tremblingly, but truly, we have yielded our hearts to Him Who died and rose again for us, saying: "Lord, Thou knowest that I was lost; but Thou hast washed my sins away, and my heart, such as it is, is given to Thee."

GOD, in His great Love, has revealed to us the SAVIOUR. We have learned, by the teaching of the HOLY GHOST, that we are CHRIST's,—not only in bright days, but when we seem forsaken; —that we are "in CHRIST" as truly, when we have toiled all the night and taken nothing, as when we see Him in the bright morning sunshine, and our nets are full. We have learned that we are joined to CHRIST, as the branches to the Vine; that we are to *receive from Him*—not, develop in ourselves—all Christian graces. In us "dwelleth no good thing." But we are "joined unto the LORD," that His strength may flow into us; that, through the outward circumstances of GOD's Providence, and through the appointed means of grace,—through prayer, and meditation on GOD's Word, and above all, through Holy Communion,—CHRIST's infinite fulness may be poured into us, the weak members of His Body. Holy Communion is a symbol of our whole Christian life: it is a *receiving*.

We have learned that there is power for the tempted, in the Passion of our LORD: power for

the life of action, and of suffering; power to "rest
in the LORD," to be "silent to the LORD."

But even now, we have not emptied the treasury of Heaven.   In CHRIST is RESURRECTION-life;
power to rejoice; power to *live,* in the highest and
truest sense.   "Because I live, ye shall live also."
Resurrection-joy is ours:—Life "more abundantly," flowing in, we know not how; Resurrection-life, to be gradually received, as He sees
fit.   We are not straitened in Him, but in ourselves.   "The arrow of the LORD's deliverance"
has been put into our hand (2 Kings xiii. 17–19).
"Smite!"   Expect still greater blessings! · Smite
six times, and six times thou shalt prevail.   But
stay thy hand, and say: "I am too weak, through
past sins, or present impotence;" smite only three
times, and thrice only shalt thou prevail.   We
are not straitened in Him, our risen SAVIOUR!

To-day, let us consider some of the ways by
which this Resurrection-life is to be realized:—
six ways by which healing virtue flows forth from
the Garment of our risen LORD.

I. If you wish to have the bright Resurrection-life *begin each day by looking at Jesus.*

One text, thought over on our knees, in the morning, links the heart to JESUS during the day. A Word of JESUS, selected in the morning, is like a flower to carry with us through the day. We may be going afterwards to business,—or to the breakfast-table,—where our temper will be tried; but we are going, not alone, but *with Jesus.*

For instance, take a text like this: "JESUS stood on the shore." St. Paul knew the meaning of this word, when he wrote: "The LORD stood with me, and strengthened me;" and St. Stephen, when he said, while those great stones were falling on him: "I see the heavens opened, and the Son of Man standing on the right hand of GOD" (St. John xxi. 4; II Tim. iv. 17; Acts vii. 56).

And try to secure a quiet *Friday,* at least in the evening: remembering the Cross of JESUS. However busy you are, from morning to night, spend—*in spirit,*—the Saturday at His Grave; end the week with JESUS. And so, the heart will be prepared for Sunday's Holy Communion;

prepared to come to Church, not to criticize—
not even to praise—the preacher, but ready to receive "things new and old." Let there be the
quiet Friday, kept in memory of His Passion;
solemn thoughts by His Tomb, on Saturday;
Easter joy repeated, every Sunday. To make
each day, each week, thus remind you of Jesus,
is the way to "rejoice in the Lord;" and "the
joy of the Lord is your strength."

II. Christian Fellowship. Let there be the
"two together."

Let us look out of ourselves, upon our brethren in Christ, struggling beside us; and, still
further, through the opened Door, on those once
struggling at our side, but now with Christ in
Paradise. Let us think of the spirits of just men
made perfect, and of the holy Angels, who are
watching us with a love which we are powerless
to conceive. Our Service is linked with theirs;
we are but one company; with Saints, and Angels, and Archangels, evermore praising God,
and saying: "Holy, Holy, Holy!"

Think of those disciples on the way to Emmaus. Two were together, talking of all that had happened, when JESUS revealed Himself to them. "While they communed together, JESUS Himself drew near, and went with them."

Think of St. John the Baptist: like a lion in the wilderness, when preaching and making converts; but, when alone in prison,—doubting! If GOD chooses for us a desolate life, He can give Easter joy in spite of it. But we lose the Easter blessing, if we choose the desolate life for ourselves. We must cultivate Christian Fellowship.

Do you say, there is a risk of "cant?" So also with the coin that is stamped with the King's image,—there is risk of counterfeit; and yet, we use it. "They that feared the LORD spake often one to another; and the LORD hearkened and heard it" (Mal. iii. 16). Speak often one to another; not of self, but of "the things pertaining to the Kingdom of GOD." Are you too "slow of speech" to be able to do this? Or is your life a lonely one? Have you no friend to whom you can thus speak? Still, look *out of self;* not only up to JESUS as the Centre, but

up to the "glorious company" around Him.
Look out of self, up to them; and forget your
individual struggles and loneliness (Heb. xii. 2,
22-24). "Praise GOD because of His Word,—
that Word which *they* found true, and which we
also shall find true, though Satan do his best to
rob us of its joy.

> "Let saints on earth in concert sing
> With those to glory gone;
> For all the servants of our King,
> In heaven and earth, are one."

III. Begin to educate yourself, from this Easter, to *do all your religious exercises as a matter of
affection* to CHRIST.

Practically, I mean this. Do not ask, "How
much time *ought* I to give to Him?" but, "How
much *may* I?" Do not say: "I *must* read my
Bible; I *must* have a quiet hour;" but say:
"*May* I have a quiet time with my FATHER in
Heaven? *May* I go out of the noise and bustle
of life, and be with HIM, for a little while? He
loves me; my LORD has promised that He will
listen if I speak to Him; that He will give me
what I ask! O what happiness! How long—

without being selfish or rude to others,—*may* I
have with my LORD? How many miles *may* I
walk with JESUS, like those two disciples?

So also, as to Intercessory Prayer. Do not
say: "*Must* I pray for others?" Say rather: "I
may pray for them; I *may* bring down blessing
on their souls, by my mid-day intercession.
There are souls that have worshipped with me,
perhaps, in this Holy Week, and do not even
know if He loves them! And He has promised,
that if I pray for them, He will hear." Of course,
their free-will can not be crushed; they may re-
ject Him again, if they choose: but He has promised to give the HOLY SPIRIT to plead with them,
if I pray. I will trust my LORD, Who loves me,
and loves them; and I will pray for them.

So let us train ourselves to say what saints say:
"I may (not, I *must*) have a quiet hour." Let
us learn to look at our religious duties as privileges, rather than obligations. Even if it cost
years to form the habit, persevere. The virtue
of CHRIST's Resurrection-power will flow in, when
this is learned.

IV. *Live by the day.*

Say to yourself: I know that my LORD would never mock me, and He says: "Take no thought for the morrow." If you want to carry Easter joy into daily life, you must be content with the day; daily grace, daily manna. How often I have had to give that advice! And how often I have forgotten to act on it myself! Day by day! Leave to-morrow, till to-morrow comes.

The widow, the ruined man, etc., instead of allowing themselves to be overwhelmed with the future, must act for the day. So also in the spiritual life. Satan tempts you by saying: "It will not last, this Easter joy. Look back on your past Easters. It is only a happy enthusiasm. It will soon be over!"—Satan's old device!—All "to-morrow," you see:—taking thought for "the morrow!" GOD will give you fresh grace to-morrow, if you live to need it. "But I shall fall again to-morrow," you say. Then, CHRIST will raise you up again, to-morrow, as He has done in the past. "JESUS CHRIST, the Same yesterday, and to-day, and forever." Of all the Lenten teaching that you have had this year, you need especially to lay to heart and cherish this: "*If you die fighting, you die saved.*"

V. *Anticipate the victory.*

Treat Satan as conquered. Do not grow disheartened when the conquered Devil, or the conquered old nature, rises up again for a moment. "Who shall separate us from the Love of CHRIST? We are more than conquerors."

A child taken in its father's arms to see a lion, at first shrinks back: "Father, I am afraid; it will kill us." But the father points out the strength of those iron bars; he shows the child that the lion has been conquered; and is bound.

It is often useful, in the spiritual warfare, to deal with Satan with a calm *satire.* When the old besetting sin comes up again,—that cowardice, or that wretched self-consciousness, or that vanity; or when that bad temper has broken out again, and Satan says: "You were mistaken, you see;"—what then?

Look at Satan with the calm spirit with which one of a conquering race would look at some wretched native, tempting him from allegiance to his King. Say to Him: "What, *you*, Satan, whom my King has conquered?—You, whose character has been exposed, as a deceiver of men? You, who were conquered on that Easter Day? You, with your wretched power, less than that of the conquered lion!—shall *you* come to *me*, who belong to the conquering Army? Get thee *behind* me, Satan!"

Try to realize your position. "Reckon ye yourselves to be dead indeed unto sin, but alive unto GOD, through JESUS CHRIST our LORD" (Rom. vi. 11). Our lower nature,—that part of us which sins,—died, in CHRIST. But the higher part of us is united with the Omnipotent; to be filled, as we can bear it, with His Fulness (see II Kings iv. 3–6; St. John i. 16; Eph. iii. 14–19). If you wish the joy of the LORD to be your strength, praise GOD because of His Word,—not because of your own feelings. Say to yourself: "This lower nature, which I hate, will die: nail after nail will be driven into it, till it dies. But the higher nature will live."

If a physician whom we trust says to us: "Times of pain will come. Be prepared for

this. Do not lose heart; they are only signs of
returning health; proofs that the disease is making the last struggle. There must be these at-
tacks of pain; but the disease is practically cured;
I stake my reputation on it." What then? At
first, when the pain returns, we are disheartened.
But, by degrees, each pain, by proving the physician true, increases our confidence in his ver-
dict of final recovery.

So with this lower nature. Our LORD has
promised victory. It is not to be won, of
course, in one short Lent! But the victory is
sure, if only we "abide" in Him; if, when
tempted, we meditate on His Love, or stay a
quarter of an hour on our knees, saying: "Glory
be to the Father," etc., or simply the Holy
Name of JESUS.

There is a mighty power in anticipation, when
we can not pray, or feel. Abound in Thanksgiving (St. Mark xi. 24; Phil. iv. 6). "Praise
GOD, because of His Word."

If you can not as yet realize "the Forgiveness
of sins," plead with Him, His own Word of
Promise. *Thou hast said*, "Though your sins

be as scarlet, they shall be as white as snow."
Thou hast said: "The Blood of JESUS CHRIST
cleanseth us from all sin." Thanks be to Thee,
because Thou hast *said* this.—And, as the soul
thus honors GOD, before all the glorious, Company of Heaven, the HOLY SPIRIT whispers with
a power never to be forgotten: "GOD is true."

When the way is dark, and you fear that you
are going to be conquered, remember the story
in the book of Chronicles: "When they began
to sing and to praise, the LORD set ambush-
ments," etc. (II Chron. xx). Praise Him thus,
now, for the victory anticipated; and one day
you shall praise Him for the victory realized.

So, in dark days, take the Name of JESUS, and
the Words of JESUS. Then, let temptation come!
Be as dark and cold as you may,—for GOD al-
lows this,—but yet, praise GOD! Sing "the
Song of Moses," aloud; and the snare will often
be broken. The HOLY SPIRIT will remind you
of this Easter, and its lessons; and you will rejoice in the LORD, and find, in that joy, more
strength, than even in the severity of Lenten
discipline.

Tuesday in Easter Week.

"THE LORD THY GOD IN THE MIDST OF THEE IS
MIGHTY: HE WILL SAVE, HE WILL REJOICE OVER THEE
WITH JOY; HE WILL REST IN HIS LOVE; HE WILL JOY
OVER THEE WITH SINGING."—(Zeph. iii. 17.)

DURING these forty days, the LORD our GOD was
in the midst of His Church; saving, rejoicing
over His disciples, resting quietly in His Love.
This is the key-note of the forty days. The Cross
was gone; the bitterness of Calvary was over; and
our LORD was in the midst of His "brethren,"
rejoicing with the calm and solemn joy of the
Incarnate GOD.

Reverently let us draw near, and ask: *What
were the elements of this joy?*

["Come, HOLY GHOST, our souls inspire;"
that the words may be few and reverent! Open
our hearts that we may see something of the
Heart of JESUS CHRIST, during those forty days
of His Resurrection-Life!]

I. Some of us have known the joy of *comfort-ing* others; of calming the fears of those who are in trouble and anxiety; of seeing the smile come through the mourner's tears. Or we have watched the mother's joy in comforting her child.

All through these forty days, JESUS had the joy of comforting His disciples. "Be not afraid." "All power is given unto Me." "Why weepest thou?" "Peace be unto you." "Why are ye troubled, and why do thoughts arise in your hearts?"—Such sympathy, alike for mind and heart! "Peace be unto you"—runs through all these forty days. The joy of *comforting* was one element of His joy.

So now also. He is nearer than the mother to her child. He knows all our difficulties and sorrows; He rejoices to remove our difficulties, —to smooth our sorrows. O the tender joy of JESUS, when some poor soul that has been dread-ing death, though loving Him, and longing to be holy, finds the sting gone, and the bed of death softer than any bed hitherto! I have often watched such a one, and have thought of the joy that is in store for that soul; as when "JESUS stood on the shore," that bright morning, after the night of fruitless toil. I can picture the joy of that soul; but oh! I can never picture the joy of JESUS! All through this troubled, tempest-tossed life, He says to us: "Be not afraid." O the joy of JESUS, when He shall have wiped away all tears from our eyes forever!

II. The joy of *helping.*

The joy of comforting is only one side of the joy of JESUS, in His Resurrection. "Comforting" is *woman's* mission, especially: and in one sense, it is the noblest mission. But CHRIST'S Human Nature was *perfect:*—the perfection of man's nature, and of *woman's* nature also. We need no Virgin Mary, to intercede!

There is a side of love, different from cheering and comforting. We can understand the joy of the Teacher over some dull boy struggling to receive a truth, as that truth at last enters in. We can conceive the joy of Bishop Selwyn, when some of his converts began to be fit for Ordination as native missionaries. We can realize the joy of a Pastor, when his teaching is laying hold of his people; when he sees them growing in grace, and beginning to be actuated by a nobler spirit; no longer asking: "How much *must* I give?"—but "How much *may* I give?" Why then should we not enter into the joy that JESUS CHRIST must have felt during those forty days, when He found the minds of His disciples opening, to understand the Scriptures; when He found that the lessons of that Holy Week had been really learned? What joy to find Peter humbled, and Thomas believing!

It is a picture of what JESUS is feeling, even now. If we ourselves are glad to be doing better, our gladness is nothing to His. He puts our tears into His bottle; He notes in His blessed "Book of remembrance," how that young girl made some sacrifice for Him; how that young man spoke out boldly for Him; how the once niggardly man is trying to give, even beyond his power; how some of us are rising to true Easter joy,—beginning to believe that He does really love us.

O the Joy of JESUS, this very day, as He looks into any of our hearts, and sees growth in grace!

When we are tempted to feel that we *must* be given up, because we are such bad pupils, what a comfort to feel that *His* joy would be lessened thereby! "How shall I give thee up, Ephraim?" (Hosea xi. 8.) "I have rejoiced over you,— loved you,—borne with you, so long! I *can not* give you up!"—O the joy that JESUS feels, in every up-rising of our regenerate nature!

III. Realized *triumph.* During these forty days, we find a vein of calm, assured victory, pervading all. There is no Gethsemane, now! "Lo, I am with you alway." It is the joy of triumph. Like Moses, on the shore of the Red Sea, when he saw the enemy dead upon the sea-shore; like Joshua, when the walls of Jericho had fallen; like a captain who is proud of his soldiers, —so the LORD JESUS CHRIST looked on His disciples, with a joy that no words can express. True, Judas was gone; but the Eleven were true to Him, and the band of holy women were true to Him. So He looked on them, as the conqueror on his great army (St. Luke x. 18; Rev. xv. 2, 3). He had won peace, by the fire of a conflict, a suffering, almost *too* strong! But now, Satan had been crushed beneath His feet; and His victory was theirs.

He looked *onward*, as He beheld that little band: and He saw the 1800 years after His Ascension, passing before Him as a dream,—a parenthesis, on the way to that great Eternity of peace and joy, when He should be recognized as the Conqueror of the Universe, and then,— deliver up this Kingdom to His FATHER!

I have often spoken of the pain that we give Him, when we will not try to do right; but think of His joy, when looking forward! He sees His Church tempted, now; but He knows that the victory is certain. "The gates of hell shall not prevail against it." That girl,—that young man, amid manifold temptations,—He sees them al- ready amid the great company standing around the Throne, with the palm-branches of triumph, singing glory to GOD!

He sees all this, and rejoices. And He saw it all, during those forty days; and His own joy so impregnated the hearts of His disciples, that, when He ascended, although they lost sight of

their truest Friend, there was no mourning.
"They worshipped Him, and returned to Jeru-
salem with great joy; and were continually in the
Temple, praising and blessing God."

O the joy that the LORD JESUS feels, this
Easter-tide, as He looks on one and another of
you, dear people, and sees *you*,—in that glorious
land, spotless before the Throne,—recognizes
you there, among those who have conquered by
faith!

There is great strength in all this; it is no mere
passing enthusiasm, but a quiet strength for the
day of darkness and difficulty. There is power
in this thought,—that JESUS loves us, and sees
us, in anticipation, "more than conquerors,
through Him that loved us."

IV. The joy of *saving*.

We have seen JESUS, with the tenderest woman's love, *comforting* His people. We have
seen His joy as a great *Teacher*, unfolding to us,
as we can bear it, the manifold mysteries of the
world unseen. We have seen Him, with the joy
of a mighty *Captain*, leading us on to certain vic-

tory.   And this "joy of the LORD" should be our "strength."

But the deepest joy with which the Heart of our dear LORD was filled, in these forty days, has not yet been touched upon: the joy of *saving*. Very few words will suffice.   The subject is not new, to some of you.

It has often been said, that the greatest saints, who for many years have disciplined the lower nature, so that they live with CHRIST in Heavenly Places (Eph. ii. 6), though they walk among us outwardly,—find the truth of our LORD's words: "It is more blessed to give than to receive." And the One Perfect Man seems to have often used those words.   In the Early Church, they appear to have reminded each other of them, when tempted to be selfish.   "*Remember* the words of the LORD JESUS, how He said: It is more blessed to give than to receive."

Picture the joy of Joseph, with his noble heart of chivalry, when about to reveal himself to his brethren !   They had almost killed him; and he was going to punish them, by giving them the land of Goshen;—by the greatness of his love !

He waited; there was a pause; he rested in his love with the joy that a noble heart feels, when going to make some one happy.—"Come near to me, I pray you. I am Joseph your brother, whom ye sold into Egypt. Be not grieved, nor angry with yourselves, that ye sold me hither; for God did send me before you,—to save your lives by a great deliverance" (Gen. xlv. 4–7).

It is a faint picture of the spirit that seems to flow out from our dear LORD, during these forty days. He rejoiced over their future work, their future sacrifices for GOD, their victories. He loved them all; but Mary Magdalene, He calls by her name; and Thomas, the doubting one; and "Simon, son of Jonas!" (St. John xx. 16, 29; xxi. 15.) See Him looking at Peter; resting in His love! "How nearly," He seems to say, "had I lost thee! How have I prayed for thee! How do I love thee, as one given back to Me!"

This is not irreverent. We must try to enter into His Heart of Love. He rejoices over all the hundred sheep; but most of all, over the one that was lost! His greatest joy is when some poor wretched sinner comes to Him as an empty vessel, to be filled;—comes, with a life wasted, confessing: "I have sinned." His greatest joy is over the lost sheep of the hundred,—over the soul that comes to Him in its emptiness. Then, the joy of the LORD is fulfilled,—His joy as SA- VIOUR. For then, the LORD can come and pour into that soul the abundance of His grace.

And therefore, as the conclusion of the whole matter, if we wish to make our LORD rejoice, this Easter-tide, we must try to bring Him many souls, that He may give them His own joy and peace;—that He may have the joy of *saving* them.

The man who has lost the wife he loved, can picture the agony of joy that it would have been to him, if, when that pulse had almost ceased to beat, a miracle of healing had been wrought, and the wife given back to his love, from the gates of death. The father and mother can remember that solemn night, when prayer was answered, and life restored to their sick child, and their hands were clasped in a joy too deep for utterance.

We can picture their joy: but no human meta- phor can make us understand the joy of our

LORD, if, to-night, He shall hear one soul that
has been wandering and doubting, say:

"Just as I am,—Thy Love, I own,
   Has broken every barrier down;
  ,Now, to be Thine, yea, Thine alone,
     O LAMB of GOD, I come!"

It is not merely the Angels that rejoice; their
joy is nothing to *His*, as He rejoices even more
over the one lost sheep, that could only *receive*
His Love, than over the ninety and nine who
have been trying for years to *give* unto Him,
their best, their all!

The LORD our GOD is in the midst of us;
mighty to save! May He rejoice over us, this
Easter with "the joy of saving"—*many* souls!
May He "see of the travail of His Soul, and—
be satisfied!"

THE POWER OF SUFFERING:

A THOUGHT FOR HOLY WEEK.

———0———

BY THE REV. GEORGE H. WILKINSON, M.A.,
Vicar of St. Peter's, Eaton Square.

———0———

IF we try to think what part of our LORD's Life it is that has influenced us, and influenced the future of His Church the most, we shall find that it is not so much what He did, as what He suffered.

From the pierced Side came the Blood and Water, for the healing of Humanity. When He was well and strong, in the human sense, He healed the sick and worked miracles; but *the power* of His Life was in His suffering and dying.

One new thought which Christianity has brought into the world is this:—the strange power that there is in Suffering.

It almost seems as if the members of CHRIST's Body are to do yet more through their suffering, than through all their energizing;—as if—we would say it reverently—through the wounds of the members, as well as of the Head, Life is to flow out !

In some ways, we can easily understand the use

of Suffering: (1) to remind us of sin; (2) to discipline us; (3) to manifest the power of the HOLY GHOST in supporting us; (4) to unite us more closely to CHRIST; (5) to develop our sympathy and love; (6) to train us for helping others.

But it appears as if it were yet more than this. St. Paul speaks as if he felt that he had to "fill up" *his part* of something that still had to be supplied, in "the afflictions of CHRIST!" (Col. i. 24).   It seems as if, in some mysterious way, the great work that CHRIST had to accomplish, with all its mysterious influence on worlds unknown to us,— as if all the benefits of CHRIST's "full, perfect, and sufficient Sacrifice" could not be received by His Church, till the wounds in *our* hands were so made, that healing could flow forth from them!

How wonderful it is, as years roll on, to watch the results of the prayer offered in faith, without feeling, by some one too weak in body and in soul to do more than say: "O GOD, remember the Covenant which Thou hast made, through JESUS CHRIST my LORD!   I pray in the Name of Thy SON JESUS CHRIST."

O the force of those hours when we are too exhausted to work, too dark and lifeless to realize any thing!   O the power of such times, not only on our own life, and on the education of the holy

Angels, but in fulfilling His Work ! The idea seems too great for us to grasp.

What hinders us in grasping it is this thought: "Yes, but JESUS CHRIST was without *sin*, and I am full of sin. How can I know that I am linked with CHRIST, in this suffering? Perhaps I am not bearing my cross—*i. e.*, the daily cross in little things—in a right way?" Satan says: "If you were pure and holy, then you might perhaps feel that you were helping in the great work; but how can you feel this, when you are so sinful, sinking beneath your cross?"

There is deep teaching for us in that story recorded by St. John, where we read of CHRIST washing His disciples' feet. They could not bear to see CHRIST *humbled :* it perplexed them. But He answered : "What I do, thou knowest not now, but thou shalt know hereafter." And now, we see that the most glorious part of His work on earth was His humiliation !

And in like manner, there is a something in the humiliations which we receive, from the assaults of Satan, from the hard and unloving world, and from our lower self rising up again and again, and even conquering us,—there is a something in all this, which, humbly borne, in darkness and in weariness, simply clinging to our LORD, may be working out untold blessings for mankind.

But, be that as it may, we are never so near to our LORD, as when He seems far away; when we are perplexed; when the old passages of the Bible have no meaning for us; when the old prayers bring no comfort; when our only language is the cry of Gethsemane: "O my Father, if it be possible, let this cup pass from me," or the cry from out of the darkness of Calvary: "My GOD, my GOD, why hast Thou forsaken me?"

O dear people, drink in,—during this Holy Week, *drink in* strength for any dark days that may be coming. Try to grasp new thoughts: write down, this Holy Week, thoughts that may come back to you, when no human presence *can* help.   Learn, so as never yet you have learned, how weakness and exhaustion—aye, even defeat —bring us nearer to HIM who, for our sake, .came to be "despised and rejected of men," the "'Man of Sorrows;" and from whose Sufferings and Death flows out the Stream of Life in which our souls are healed.

E. P. DUTTON & CO., PUBLISHERS, NEW YORK.
Price $1.50 a hundred copies.

BY THE REV. G. H. WILKINSON, M.A.

HOLY WEEK AND EASTER.
   MEDITATIONS FOR EACH DAY. Square, 16mo. Paper, 25 cents; cloth, 50 cents.

THE POWER OF SUFFERING:
   A THOUGHT FOR HOLY WEEK. Leaflet, per hundred, $1.50.

HOW TO KEEP LENT.
   A QUINQUAGESIMA SUNDAY ADDRESS. From the Fifth Thousand of English Edition. Paper, 10 cents; per hundred, $8.00.

SOME WEEK DAYS IN LENT.
   Paper, 25 cents; cloth, 50 cents.
   "Plain, earnest, and thorough,—good for distribution, and worth the attention of the clergy as models of style and method in the pulpit."

BE YE RECONCILED TO GOD.
   Paper, 5 cents.

BREAK UP YOUR FALLOW GROUND.
   A HELP TO SELF-EXAMINATION. Paper, 10 cents.

COME TO THE MISSION.
   A LEAFLET FOR DISTRIBUTION AT MISSION SERVICES. Price, per hundred, $1.00.

INSTRUCTIONS IN THE WAY OF SALVATION.
   Paper, 25 cents. (Eighteen Thousand of English Edition sold.)

GUIDE TO A DEVOUT LIFE.
   BEING COUNSELS TO THE CONFIRMED. Eighth Thousand. Paper, 25 cents; cloth, 50 cents. (Forty-two Thousand of English Edition have been sold.)
   "A carefully systematized plan of directions, which for sound sense and real piety, we have never seen equaled."—*An English Church Paper.*
   "Will be found to be among the very best and most useful of devotional books." *The Churchman.*
   "It is, without exception, the best book of the kind I have ever seen, and i would be difficult, it seems to me, for any one to make a better."—*A City Rector*

E. P. DUTTON & CO., Publishers, New York.

HELPS TO A HOLY LENT.

By the Rt. Rev. F. D. Huntington, D.D., Bishop of Central New York. Fifth Thousand. 208 pages. Paper, 30; cloth, 50 cents. "A rich treasury filled with beautiful, living thoughts, the power and attraction of which will be confessed by all who give the work due examination." *Churchman.*

NEW HELPS TO A HOLY LENT.

By the Rt. Rev. F. D. Huntington, D.D. 16mo, 288 pp., $1.25.

READINGS FOR EVERY DAY IN LENT.

Compiled from the writings of Bishop Jeremy Taylor. By Miss Sewell. 16mo, 360 pp., price reduced to $1.25.

DEAR FEAST OF LENT.

A SERIES OF DEVOTIONAL READINGS. Arranged by the author of "A Rosary for Lent," etc. 16mo, beveled boards, red edges, $1.00.

ROSARY FOR LENT;

OR, DEVOTIONAL READINGS, ORIGINAL AND COMPILED. By the author of "Rutledge." New Edition, $1.50.

THOUGHTS FOR LENT.

By the Rt. Rev. Ashton Oxenden, D.D. 16mo, 105 pp., red edges, 75 cents.

THE SEASON OF LENT.

A COMPANION FOR THE CLOSET. By the Rt. Rev. George D. Gillespie, D.D. Paper, 10 cents.

DAILY HYMNS;

OR, HYMNS FOR EVERY DAY IN LENT. Paper, 30 cents; cloth, gilt edge, 60 cents.

GOOD·FRIDAY ADDRESSES

ON THE SEVEN LAST WORDS OF OUR LORD. By the Rev. G. H. Houghton, S.T.D., Rector of the Church of the Transfiguration, New York. Cloth, red edges, 50 cents.

HOLY WEEK.

THE EVENTS OF THE LAST WEEK OF OUR SAVIOUR'S LIFE, in leaflet form. Twenty-first Thousand. Paper, 4 pp., per hundred, $1.50.

THOUGHTS FOR HOLY WEEK.

By Miss Sewell. New Edition. 184 pp., cloth, 40 cents.

THE DAILY ROUND.

MEDITATION, PRAYER, AND PRAISE, adapted to the Course of the Christian Year. With an Introduction and other additions by the Rt. Rev. A. C. Coxe, D.D. 32mo, 418 pp. Leatherette, red edge, $1.00. 16mo, large type, 418 pp., red edge, $1.50.

"It only needs to be known in order to secure a large circulation."—*Dean Bickersteth.*

"I am thankful for a book which I can thus commend to my diocese and to all my friends."—*Bishop Coxe.*

"Remarkable for terseness and suggestiveness of thought."—*Literary Churchman* (London).

"I am greatly struck by its resolute insistance upon the connection between devotion and practice—in other words, by its moral backbone."—*Canon Liddon.*

FOR DAYS AND FOR YEARS.

TEXT, SHORT READING, AND HYMNS FOR EVERY DAY IN THE CHURCH YEAR. Selected by H. L. Sidney Lear. 16mo, 412 pp., cloth, $1.00.

"The object of the editor of this devotional work has been to follow the spirit and teaching of the Christian year. The 'readings' have been selected from writers of every age, ancient and modern, from the early fathers, and from the divines of our own day. The hymns have been, like the readings, chosen from the richest sources; and the book, as a whole, will be cherished for its preciousness by all who use it daily. We have seen nothing of the kind superior to it." *The Churchman.*

DAILY GLEANINGS OF THE SAINTLY LIFE.

Compiled by C. M. S. With an Introduction by the Rev. M. F. Sadler. Scripture Text, Reading, and Hymn for Every Day of the Church Year. 16mo, 400 pp., $1.25.

MANUAL OF DEVOTION FROM THE WRITINGS OF ST. AUGUSTINE.

Translated by the Rev. Marcus Dods, D.D. 16mo, cloth, red edges, $1.00.

STEPS TO CHRISTIAN MANHOOD.

A BOOK FOR YOUNG MEN. By R. Marryat, with an Introduction by the Rev. Henry C. Potter, D.D. 127 pp., paper, 30 cents. 127 pp., cloth, 50 cents.

THE LIFE OF FAITH.

MEDITATIONS FROM THE FRENCH. With a Preface by the Rev. Morgan Dix, S.T.D. Paper, 10 cents; cloth, 25 cents.

· E. P. DUTTON & CO., Publishers, New York.

HE GIVETH SONGS.

A COLLECTION OF RELIGIOUS LYRICS.

By W. M. L. JAY, A. E. HAMILTON, AND OTHERS. WITH
ILLUSTRATIONS BY L. B. HUMPHREY.
16MO, GILT, $1.25.

"This is a choice volume without and within, attractive to the eye
and restful to the thought. Some of the deepest and richest spiritual
experiences have found expression in verse, and collections like this
are the fruitage of much true and noble living. Many of the poems
are from the pen of Miss Hamilton, and are as full of poetic beauty
as of thought, and feeling. Peace and trust are of the chords oftenest
struck, and their music is always comforting and helpful."—*The
Christian Union.*

"The compiler of the exquisite little book of religious lyrics, 'He
Giveth Songs,' has the credit of introducing to American readers a
new poet, Miss Anna E. Hamilton. Her poems are original in style
and conception, for the most part short, but always tersely, often
exquisitely, expressed."—*N. Y. Times.*

"This collection of devotional poetry is remarkably fresh, nor is
it wanting in merit. In fact, we should not hesitate to place this
volume among the best of its class. A considerable portion of the
songs here printed are from the pen of the author of 'Shiloh,' a
woman of rare poetic power, and one whose verses are destined to
grow constantly in popular favor. The volume will serve most ap-
propriately as a gift. But, at the same time, it is a book which every
reader will want to keep for himself, for it contains some of the best
religious poetry we have ever seen."—*Churchman.*

"Here is an attempt to bring together the choicest of the brief
religious lyrics which have come from our Church writers. It is the
choicest volume of religious poetry which we have ever seen, and
the book itself, so far as the printer's and engraver's and binder's art
is concerned, is as beautiful as the gems within it. You can discount
most collections like this by fifty per cent., but here the quality is
that of pure gold. There is no alloy, and the publishers have once
for all issued a book of this sort for which one can only say 'Thanks.'
It is choice, even exquisite from cover to cover, and covers included."
Standard of the Cross.

E. P. DUTTON & CO., Publishers, New York.